The Safe House

The
SAFE
HOUSE

A Novel

Christophe Boltanski

Translated by Laura Marris

THE UNIVERSITY OF CHICAGO PRESS

Chicago and London

The University of Chicago Press, Chicago 60637
The University of Chicago Press, Ltd., London
© 2017 by The University of Chicago
Published 2017
Printed in the United States of America

26 25 24 23 22 21 20 19 18 17   1 2 3 4 5

ISBN-13: 978-0-226-44919-7 (cloth)
ISBN-13: 978-0-226-44922-7 (e-book)
DOI: 10.7208/chicago/9780226449227.001.0001

Originally published as *La cache*. © Éditions Stock, 2015
Illustrations by Mickaël De Clippeleir

The University of Chicago Press gratefully acknowledges
the generous support of the France Chicago Center toward
the translation and publication of this book.

Library of Congress Cataloging-in-Publication Data

Names: Boltanski, Christophe, author. | Marris, Laura, 1987– translator.
Title: The safe house : a novel / Christophe Boltanski ; translated by
    Laura Marris.
Other titles: Cache. English (Marris)
Description: Chicago ; London : The University of Chicago Press, 2017.
    | Originally published in French: Paris : Stock, 2015 under title:
    La cache : roman. | Includes bibliographical references and index.
Identifiers: LCCN 2017008988 | ISBN 9780226449197 (cloth : alk. pa-
    per) | ISBN 9780226449227 (e-book)
Subjects: LCSH: Boltanski, Christophe—Family—Fiction. | LCGFT:
    Fiction. | Novels.
Classification: LCC PQ2662.O5712 C3313 2017 | DDC 843/.914—dc23
    LC record available at https://lccn.loc.gov/2017008988

♾ This paper meets the requirements of ANSI/NISO
z39.48-1992 (Permanence of Paper).

FOR ANNE AND JEAN-ÉLIE

Contents

Car

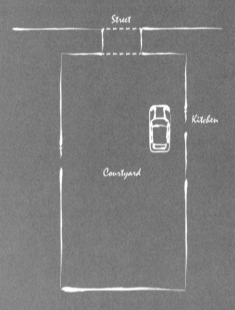

Street

Kitchen

Courtyard

1

I never saw them walk outside alone. Or even together. Never saw them so much as stroll the length of a block. They only ventured out on wheels. Sitting pressed against each other, shielded by the body of the car—behind some cover, no matter how slight. In Paris, they drove around in a Fiat 500 Lusso, a white one. It was a simple car, easy to handle, reassuring. It suited their scale, round and dwarf sized, with its speedometer that went up to seventy-five miles per hour, its two-cylinder rear engine making a death rattle, the sputter of an old, hacking tugboat. They parked it in the cobblestone courtyard facing the archway, along the main wing of the house, ready to leave at a moment's notice, almost stuck to the wall like the escape pod of a rocket ship. The front passenger door always opposite the kitchen entrance. They only had to navigate a few stone stairs to reach their vehicle, and to make it easier, an extra step had been added to part of each stair at half height. Once they made it down, they could drop straight into the car. No one was abandoned—we always left together. She would take the wheel. He'd sit next to her. I piled into the backseat with Anne and Jean-Élie.

She wore huge glasses with clear brown frames and slightly tinted oval lenses. Before turning the ignition, she would lean toward the mirror on the back of the visor, fluff her hair with her palms to lift it into a pouf, stick out her cheeks, and make a duck-faced pout to check her foundation and lipstick. Then she'd start the engine with a racket like a bunch of pots and pans reverberating off the facades. At the helm of her little motor, which was seized with violent trembling every time the pistons turned, she morphed into a cyborg. One with her machine.

Since her lifeless legs couldn't press the pedals, long levers had been added with the help of God-knows-what mechanic. Like the broom handles from vintage airplanes, these allowed her to brake and accelerate—and so to drive, which she did at considerable speed, at her fastest whenever she encountered a pedestrian crossing against the light. She pounced with joyful rage, preferably on limping old men, to punish them for what little freedom of movement they had and to scare her passengers. She never ran anyone over. I have no idea if she had a license, and if so, by what means she had gotten one. She loved driving. The car was her wheelchair, her legs regained, her triumph over forced immobility.

2

When had they stopped walking in the streets? In her case, I know. During the early thirties. Ever since she contracted polio in medical school, not long after Jean-Élie was born. Because of her stubborn refusal to use crutches, to be seen publicly as a feeble person, deprived of a part of herself. Once, when a waiter in a restaurant hurried to hold the door for her, she shouted that she didn't need anyone's help. She hated false pity, the smug kindness the seemingly healthy show to those who aren't. But what about him? When did he decide to stop going to work on foot? To give up strolling along the quays, browsing through the booksellers' stalls? To stop running errands? To live without a cent in his pocket? To boycott public transportation? Never to sit alone at a sidewalk café or even set foot outside without company? Was it his choice or his wife's? Was he suffering from some acute form of agoraphobia? Did he, in snubbing a natural form of human locomotion, want to show his sympathy—or even his love—for a woman at war with the laws of mechanics?

She was his chauffeur. She dropped him off in front of official buildings hewn from stone, watched him disappear through monumental doors topped with the tricolored flag. Then she staked out his return. She drove him everywhere, as if he were a wounded hero. To the hospital, when he still practiced, to committees where he discussed disability and impairment, to scholarly conferences on the handicapped. In the middle of the night, with their sleeping children in tow, she drove him to the bedsides of the dying, or more frequently, of hypochondriacs. Without his escort, he would surely have been lost. This conscientious doctor, adored by his patients, showered with diplomas, honors, decorations, was like a child, naked in front of the dressed. By turns happy, tormented, anguished, he moved through the world without a fallback, defenseless as a hermit crab pulled from its shell, left to the mercy of the first passing predator. Incapable of lying or concealing his emotions, he could burst into sobs at the slightest hint of feeling. A book, a piece of music, an offhand remark—these were enough to make him weep or blush to the tips of his ears.

His large head, his strong neck, his high forehead and flattish skull, his sparse, close-cropped hair—physically, he looked a little like Erich von Stroheim without the Prussian stiffness. In public, his persona had nothing in common with the actor's noble yet sadistic soldiering, but his pose was equally contrived in its own way—the English gentleman, at once delicate, modest, and reserved. To this end, he sported a thin mustache, parted like David Niven's, always wore a beige woolen vest under his jacket, smoked a briar pipe, the straight-stemmed, average model, typically made in Saint-Claude, and he affected a taste for scotch, though he almost never drank. With long, almond-shaped eyes exaggerated by well-defined lashes, he gazed around with an air of perpetual astonishment, as if the whole world remained a mystery. We protected him, banding together, threading around his form. Whatever happened, we were his bodyguards. His air bags, ready to inflate at the slightest shock.

3

The second-generation Fiat Nuova 500 was an icon in Italian films of the fifties, but it reminded me of a goldfish bowl, a three-man submarine, a UFO—and I, its passenger, a Martian launched onto an unknown planet. In Italy, they called it the *bambina*. The French, less inclined to flatter, nicknamed it the "yogurt tub." Its floor scraped the ground. Its sheeting was thin as tinfoil. In the back, the absence of rear doors or even moveable rear windows heightened the sense of entrapment. I sometimes spent hours with my rump against the motor, my senses jangled by each throb, my body doubled up, knees wedged against the front seat, face pressed against the porthole, watching the blackened buildings roll by in one low-angle shot, a monotonous landscape blurred by condensation. Deafened by the engine, I traversed wide arteries coated with soot—the rue Bonaparte, the boulevard Morland, the avenue de Ségur, the rue de Sèvres, the rue Vaneau, the avenue du Maine—in a weightless state, as if I were moving through a dim watery world (and don't they say traffic is fluid?)—a world of ink blots, of deep-sea trenches filled with transparent fish. I huddled in a fetal position inside that ovoid vessel, that rolling womb piloted by my grandmother, visible to everyone and yet curiously unseen amid the commotion of the city.

They lived in one of those mansions that were usually named after a marquis or a viscount, midway down the rue de Grenelle. As strangers to nobility and everything it represented, they had nothing to do with their Saint-Germain neighborhood, which since Balzac has stood less for a part of the city than for a social class, a set of manners, an air, a way of speaking. Until age thirteen, when I decided to live with them permanently, they looked after me on days off, which was nearly half the week. On Tuesday (or was it Wednesday?) afternoons, they came to get me after class in the 14th arrondissement, rue Hippolyte-Maindron, and returned me to my mother's house on the impasse du Moulin-Vert the following night. Then they picked me up again on the weekend, from noon on Saturday until Sunday. They would all be there, waiting for me in the Fiat at the school entrance, and later, when I was in Lavoisier secondary school, from a respectful distance. With each new grade, they parked a little farther away to avoid embarrassing me in front of the other students. Rue Pierre-Nicole, then rue Feuillantines, close to Val-de-Grâce. Eventually, on a day that probably corresponded with becoming a teenager, I took the 83 bus from the Port-Royal stop—destination Bac-Saint-Germain.

In his childhood, when they had a Citroën Traction Avant, my uncle Christian spent 9:15 to 12:30 each morning sitting in the same spot while his father finished his duties at Laennec. The hospital terrified him, with its ballet of ambulances and police vans blaring their sirens. For good reason, he associated it with suffering and death. The Citroën wasn't parked in front of the main entrance, on the rue de Sèvres, but on the Vaneau side. Were they sparing him the spectacle or merely following parking regulations? And what could he do in a glass box in the middle of Paris? He took in the view. The traffic cops slipping parking tickets under windshield wipers, the acrobatics of a driver who kept trying, vainly, to fit between two bumpers, the construction workers jackhammering a sidewalk, the pigeons perching on a gutter, a strip of sky veiled by exhaust. Christian stared at the passersby. After a while, he knew them all: the old biddy in gabardine, the postman in his mail cart, the old man swallowed by his raincoat, the woman pushing a baby carriage. With his forehead against the glass, he scanned the street for the arrival of a girl he'd fallen in love with, though he never said a word to her.

He waited until adulthood before daring to go outside without this protective cocoon. He was eighteen the first time. He didn't walk far. Five hundred yards at most, between the house and a tiny gallery called Les Tournesols, which specialized in Yiddish art. His mother had opened it on the rue de Verneuil to find something for him to do. He looked after the space and painted in the back room. After a few months, he took over the direction of the gallery and started showing painters he chose himself, like Jean le Gac. I don't know if anyone came to fetch him after that first solo excursion. For several years, his parents continued to go with him in the car each time he went out. To the Académie Julian where he took drawing classes, to museums, exhibitions. My father, Luc, insists he gained his own independence earlier than Christian did. But once, at about the same age, when he expressed a desire to get some fresh air and go sailing, Luc found himself on a boat with his whole family. A single-hulled, thirty-two-foot-long sailboat moored at Graau, in Dutch Friseland. A skipper was included. How did his mother, with her unruly stems, manage to hoist herself aboard? "If he'd wanted to take a caravan across the desert," said Christian, "we would have all been mounted on camels."

5

In winter, during her long hours of waiting, she left the engine running to keep warm. She put a hot-water bottle between her knees, covered it with a plaid blanket, and blackened pages with a pen, leaning on a leather lap desk. Under the pseudonym Annie Lauran, she wrote novels about her sad, solitary childhood, about her adoption (when she was "bought") by her godmother, an eccentric society woman and patroness, about her father, a penniless, morphine-addicted lawyer from Rennes who was worn down by political defeat, about her brother, an adventurer, overcome by delusions of grandeur and exiled to French Polynesia like some Napoleon in Saint Helena. Very beautiful books set in a long-ago country of cathedrals and baptisteries in the humid and superstitious province of Mayenne, or in an overseas France, restrictive and colonial. She was also the author of quasi-sociological essays—astonishingly prescient studies of second-generation immigrants, the "children from nowhere," as she called them, or of the marginalized "third age," an expression that was popular in the seventies before the invention of senior citizens and elder rights. She advocated a "tape-recorder literature," which depended on strictly cataloging real life. Following Jean Rouch's cinéma vérité, it was a neutral style, free from any kind of psychology. She wrote about twenty books in total, published by Plon or Pierre-Jean Oswald, and later with the Éditeurs Français Réunis, the publishing house of the Communist Party, often with photographs or collages by Christian on the cover. A life's work that has unjustly fallen into oblivion.

6

After my birth, when she was forced to adjust to her new gene-alogical status by adopting a term, if not of endearment, then at least of familiarity, she chose the title mère-grand after the story of "Little Red Riding Hood," or more specifically, the Big Bad Wolf—that two-headed hydra who combines sweetness and a growling voice, innocence and predation, nightgown and gray pelt, cotton bonnet and snapping fangs. She liked to provoke people, to disrupt social codes, to seduce as she intim-idated. "Granny," the nickname chosen by my maternal grand-mother, wouldn't have suited her. She had nothing in common with those sweet old ladies cooking up cakes and jams for their descendants. No chance she'd get lumped in with the stereotyp-ical grandmas or share their penchant for benevolent smiles, indulgence, and attention lavished on naughty children under the affectionate gaze of passersby. She had a savage appetite for life. She bubbled over with the force of a pressure cooker, unable to transfer her overflowing energy into four motorized wheels. Like the animal in the fairy tale, she was confined to her bed and hollowed by raging hunger. She would have de-voured us all just the same as the little girl dressed in crimson. We had become her arms, her legs, extensions of her body.

In public spaces—the airport lobby, the terrace of a café, a movie theater, or the annual book festival for the Commu-nist newspaper *L'Humanité*, I was forbidden from calling her mère-grand or pronouncing any such formula that might re-veal her age, a subject she guarded with the utmost secrecy. As I write these words, I still don't know exactly when she was born, and I cringe from doing the necessary research with the au-thorities for fear of violating her deepest privacy. She refused, in her words, "everything that leaves a mark." Starting with the weight of years, the slow decline, the physical decay, the narrowed life that reminded her of her illness, another setback she never stopped battling. She took infinite care with her appearance. She dyed her hair a reddish black, abused self-tanning lotion, and in spite of her difficulties with mobility, wore high heels to gain a few inches. In front of strangers I had to call her "aunt," a more respectful title, and a much less temporal one, not tied to old age like the title she'd given herself, which was certainly burlesque, but not very flattering. To prevent confusion, I avoided addressing her in public.

7

Of course, we sometimes left our spaceship to go see a movie (preferably American) or to eat at a restaurant. The venues were picked for their ease of access and their anonymity. Cinemas like the Maine, the Escurial, and the MacMahon, with their theaters on the ground floor. Or big brasseries, loud and impersonal, like the Coupoule or the Select, located on either side of the boulevard Montparnasse, and also Les Ministères, an establishment on the rue du Bac. Never French bistros, with their checkered table cloths, so-called traditional cuisine, candle stubs, and solicitous proprietors. We wanted to melt into the mass of guests or spectators. Despite our efforts to stay unnoticed, I felt the weight of stares as soon as we disembarked somewhere. We made a curious team, our small figures hitched together (all skinny, with the exception of my more voluminous grandfather), our dark coloring, and our tortoise pace, our serious look, almost on guard. Hand in hand, huddled together, we formed one single being, a sort of overgrown millipede. I was obviously a little embarrassed by these creatures, so frail, so vulnerable. The wife held up from both sides, the husband leaning on a cane. We surrounded them. When I didn't offer my arm, I acted like I didn't know them—I went ahead, nose in the air. As much as I loved the warmth, the close chaos of the Fiat, I dreaded these outings in the open, those few feet to cross in front of everyone.

8

This time we were all on a mission. Sunday morning, an appropriate time for both profane and religious rituals, began with delivering *L'Humanité*. She was the card-carrying Communist. An affiliation which had more to do with her loyalty to her publisher than with an ideology that had always been a little fuzzy in her mind. Despite her handicap, she went at least once a month to pick up the weekly paper in the 7th arrondissement at the rue Amélie branch before distributing it to the few subscribers in her area. She did the driving; Jean-Élie and Anne made the deliveries. In line with the sociology of the neighborhood, the cell she belonged to included a number of executives and highly trained professionals, even CEOs with ten or more employees, as the National Institute for Statistics and Economic Research would say. The Nomenklatura of the Eastern Bloc might have been a better comparison for this strange sample of the French Communist Party. The lawyer defended the General Labor Commission, the banker managed Soviet investments in France, the poet sat on the Central Committee, the editor published her writer comrades. As residents of enemy territory, they avoided all proselytizing through flyers, leaflets, or canvassing. Securely bourgeois, but secretly militant, they carried out their political activities with great discretion. When Anne delivered the paper, they hurried to let her in and shut the door behind her, afraid a neighbor would catch them with such seditious literature. They were unsure how to treat this young woman—not quite a comrade or a fellow traveler, or even a delivery girl you offer to tip. One of them asked her if she'd like to earn a little money bringing him croissants.

After *L'Huma*, there was mass. At Saint-Sulpice. In front of it, actually, on the plaza. Neither grandparent entered the church. The roles were always the same: Jean-Élie and Anne scouting ahead, swallowed by the monumental entryway. The rest of us stayed in the car, waiting for the end of the service, seated, gathered together, prostrate at the foot of the steps, beneath the huge colonnade. The Fiat was conducive to gen-uflections. Did they get out a missal? Murmur the Hail Mary and the Our Father? Or did they pray by proxy, through their emissary children? I remember nothing but a long silence, an empty square, a fountain where no water flowed. A closed newspaper kiosk. Motionless beggars with their backs against the columns. Chairs piled behind the glass at the Café de la Mairie. Deserted parking. And I was lost in contemplation of a movie poster spread across the facade of Bonaparte Cinema, trying to decipher the film's name through rows of chestnut trees, anxiously watching for my aunt and uncle to reappear from that asymmetrical, almost lopsided edifice, eager for the bells, the signal for their deliverance and our departure.

The mornings ended in the Marais, on the rue des Rosiers, which wasn't yet that pedestrian alley invaded by boutiques and falafel shops but still a lively, working-class thoroughfare. Another ritual. We bought bread with cumin, poppy-seed cakes, and cream-cheese tart from Finkelsztajn's bakery, charcuterie and relishes from Goldenberg, Blum, or Klapisch—endlessly debating which of the three had the best pastrami, corned beef, and liverwurst—and, in a grocery with a name I've forgotten tiled in little blue squares on the rue des Hospitalières-Saint-Gervais, we bought matzo, which I gobbled down covered with butter and ham, a double violation of kosher law that made grand-papa smile. I can't remember noticing any contradictions in this long Sunday sequence. At least not until I was much older. And what did he make of it all?

9

In one of life's coincidences, his own father also had a close relationship with cars. He should have ridden in a carriage, standing with his brows arched, dressed as Mephistopheles in a red cape, making his entrance to a shower of applause. Instead, he built the carriages. He grew up in Odessa, that musically inclined town on the Black Sea. A child of the ghetto, born to a pious family of modest means, he had an incredible voice. A gay, rich merchant (or a charitable lady, depending on the version) paid for his singing lessons and told him over and over that he was the next Feodor Chaliapin. The boards of the imperial stage awaited him. He would play Boris Godunov. He would collapse in front of the czar. He would spit out the "Ah! Ah! Ah! Blacha!" in the King of England's face (a fantasy that was apparently pretty common in Russia—years later, the writer Romain Gary revealed that his mother had promised him the same future). Tuberculosis of the vocal cords put an end to his lyrical ambitions and dreams of glory. Under the combined pressure of sickness and pogroms, he immigrated to France around 1895 in hopes of a better life despite the formal degradation, that same year, of Captain Alfred Dreyfus in the grand courtyard of the École Militaire. He arrived in Paris on a Sunday. Everything was closed except a carriage shop, most likely located near the Gare de l'Est. The owner asked him what his trade was. He didn't know how to do anything except sing, and he didn't speak French. He held out his hands. And so he became an upholsterer, a maker of seats, cushions, trimmings for cars. Then he was hired as a laborer for Citroën. Was it on the quai de Javel or the place de Clichy? A tough job, with long periods of boredom and intervals of overwork. He ended up a shop foreman. As he was dying of cancer, he begged his friends to take him to one last opera. Apparently they brought him to the Palais Garnier on a stretcher. Christian was always skeptical of this story—too melodramatic to be true. According to him, his forefather's tragic career as a great bass never surpassed the role of cantor in a synagogue.

10

They covered thousands of miles on vacation, not in the Fiat 500 but in a Volvo 144, better designed for highways—hardy, square, cut from Swedish steel. They got out as little as possible, spending their days and nights in the car. To avoid lobbies, endless corridors, narrow staircases, the cramped attic rooms of hotels, mère-grand liked to sleep sitting up, in random towns, squeezed in the front seat with her people piled around her. That way she could watch over them without having to talk a suspicious receptionist into a single room for five people (including three adults). Jean-Élie sat next to her. I have no idea how he managed to sleep with the steering wheel jabbing his ribs, his head squashed against the window. A teenaged Anne lay down in the backseat. Grand-papa slept above her on a plank balanced between the headrest and the rear window ledge. When I was with them, I was sandwiched between suitcases in the trunk, which was left open so I could breathe. At the port of Brindisi, in Italy, I was once awakened by a soldier's flashlight. I still have a terrified memory of a beam passing over my face, of whispering in a language I didn't know. The officers probably suspected a theft when they noticed the gaping trunk—until they saw the outlines of our sleeping forms.

In previous years, in other cars, Christian was always in with the bags. His brother, Luc, was in Anne's spot. Their father stretched across the axle, abutting a Dutch poet with long hair, a family friend wrapped in a green cape. The combinations and actors could change—it was always the same *tableau vivant*, the same architecture—a mass of flesh and steel like the aftermath of a car wreck. We woke to ghostly parking lots and the sound of horns. In lieu of a bathroom, mère-grand hid behind the car door, perching on the running board above a commode. We rarely changed clothes. We washed ourselves like cats, with an Évian mister or a water bottle. We sneered at museums, at castles, at ruins, at beaches, at bits of greenery, at picturesque villages, at famous restaurants, at sites worth a detour. They traveled like this, without me, all the way to Iran, to the Arctic Circle, to Moscow, beyond the Tropic of Cancer. They crossed the United States from east to west, Australia from north to south. In their travels they "sacrificed depth for breadth," as Paul Morand would say. Their goal was not to explore faraway and exotic countries but to cover the longest distances possible, to stick new pins in the surface of the globe.

11

Were the drivers already out of gas, or had they also gone on strike? We rolled through a sun-drenched Paris, empty as the first day of summer vacation. Up the avenue General Leclerc. It was morning. Through the little portholes of the Fiat, the lion on the place Denfert looked like a circus animal, dabbed with bright paint. Mère-grand and Jean-Élie wore conspiratorial smiles. We passed through a city covered in graffiti and shredded posters with an overflowing bucket of paste between our feet, a broom, and our own ream of flyers. The message we were going to plaster on walls had little to do with the first tremors of May 1968. I was six then. In the alley where my parents lived I played riot police and protesters with the neighboring kids. I chose the side of law and order I think because I liked their uniforms. There was nothing about police violence on the little rectangular brown posters we were about to put up—instead they read "The Impossible Life of Christian Boltanski." I didn't understand why my uncle judged his short existence so severely or why he wanted to advertise it to the Parisian population (with the help of his family, no less). It was his first show. Henri Ginet, a friend of the surrealists, had offered his theater and cinema, the Ranelagh, named after the garden in the 16th arrondissement. Christian installed his paint-splattered chiffon mannequins at the bottom of a huge staircase in the faux-Renaissance-style lobby with its walls upholstered in red felt. I have a vivid memory of the opening—the evening of May 3, 1968. Jean-Élie arrived, full of emotion, and announced there were barricades in the Latin Quarter.

12

We backed into the courtyard, careful to avoid bumping the two little hoops of wrought iron that framed the archway. The neighbor, who'd inherited an old publishing house specializing in travel books, wanted to get rid of our old clunker. She dreamed of a French garden—elegant, rectangular, in the style of Le Nôtre at Versailles. To that end, she'd built a perpetually dry fountain on her side and planted some hawthorn bushes around it in lines that were more or less geometrical. Topiaries in spheres or cones, saplings that all ended up stunted and scrawny for lack of sunshine. She would have liked to identify her property with a particular century (preferably the seventeenth) to classify this very particular mansion—damp in winter, cool in summer, always in the shade, melancholy, full of dusty, grainy air—and better yet, to designate its style, endow it with a prestigious name. But she was rejected without appeal by the board of historic preservation. The building was a bric-a-brac of architectural styles, a heap of geological strata, a patchwork of different eras that had lumped a seventeenth-century rotunda in with an ivy-smothered Louis-the-fifteenth facade and many more recent additions.

It might seem strange to begin the description of a house with its car. But just like her Swedish older sister, the Fiat 500 was the first room of the Rue-de-Grenelle, an extension, an airlock, a removable part, a space beyond its walls, a pair of eyes or at least an eyeball. Like the foyer, it formed a finite universe, round, smooth, as warm and reassuring as a hearth. It wasn't just a mode of transportation—it was a habitat. At once empty, transparent, and full as an egg; open glass surfaces and closed, locked doors, watertight rubber seals and nickel plating. The interior was defined by its opposite, that urban backdrop, ever-present and yet faraway, unreal. It satisfied our need for evasion, for confinement, for going out into the world yet retreating into our unborn state. It stood for the female body, protector and midwife. A symbol that was as phallic as it was maternal—as much *domus* as *domina*, domicile and dominator. Mère-grand furnished it with useful objects: hairbrush, Bic pens, makeup-remover towelettes called Quickies, tissues, sunglasses, gold-foil packets of 555 cigarettes in the style of Blaise Cendrars, another maimed artist who transformed his Alfa Romeo into a moving bedroom, filling his glove compartment with chapters from books he wanted to read.

13

I can imagine the look of rage on her face when she found, on her windshield, the wide-ruled sheet of paper covered in block letters that read: "PROFFESSOR BOLTANSKI JEW." Right away she recognized the childish handwriting not just because of the spelling mistake and the awkward pettiness of the expression. She had no trouble confronting the culprit. One day, in a honeyed tone, she asked him, "Sweetie, how do you spell professor?" The boy was barely older than I was—neat, well behaved, in short trousers, his hair parted on the side, and he hurried to answer her. Did she ask afterward for an explanation from his parents, who were also perfect—in navy-blue ensembles, with blazer, pleated skirt, and headband to match—and lived on the second floor? She kept repeating that this label, which crawled out of the night, hadn't just "occurred to him." He would have heard hints and rumors around his family's dinner table about "those people next door," about that man who put the title "professor" on his mailbox, hints and rumors he might have shared at Saint-Something-or-Other school with his many classmates in the neighborhood. Did one of them suggest the act? To unmask the intruder? While she railed, not against the child but against the hate-molded society that he'd come from, the message's intended recipient said nothing. A sheet of paper, three words, brought it all back.

14

How do they get to the police station? Not in Hotchkiss, that car with the tapered front he was so proud of despite its many breakdowns. The German army had already seized it. Not on foot, despite the short distance. Probably in the Vélocar, which at that point hadn't yet been confiscated. This four-wheel bike, with its lightweight body, had already caused him some trouble. After buying it from a stranger, he was accused of theft by a youngster in the neighborhood who pretended to be the owner. Of course he paid him what he asked. He was in no position to argue.

Arriving at 10 rue Perronet, he helps his wife, with him as always, to navigate the dusty staircase. His mother, who has also been summoned, brings up the rear. The police station occupies two floors of a masonry building on the corner. They are one of the first groups to get their patches. Those whose names began with *A* or *B* were called on Tuesday, June 2, 1942. A man wearing a threadbare suit admits them to a murky, smoke-filled room. He politely offers a chair to the handicapped wife but not to the mother. The two outcasts stand, facing the police officer as he sits behind his desk. Was he the same one who listed them in a special registry in October 1940? The one who said, as though it were obvious, "Monsieur Boltanski, there's another Jew who lives near you, a Mr. Levy. I'm sure you know him?" He gives each of them the yellow square, with three stars to cut out with scissors, and asks them to sign the column that serves as a roster. In exchange, he demands a textile coupon from their ration books. His mother emerges first, her eyes wide, the cloth in her hand, which she'll cut once she gets home, following the black line, and apply with care to the lapels of her coats. On

the sidewalk, she breaks down. Seeing the scrap of fabric
the tears on her face, a passing woman embraces her and s___
"From now on, we'll know who our real friends are!"

15

He wears his yellow mark. She huddles at his side. He pedals as
fast as he can through the partially deserted city. They almost
never go out anymore, but they've been notified of a shipment.
Oranges. Impossible to find. A whole crate. Where do they go to
get it? Jean-Élie can't remember. "Maybe a train station." And
who's the sender? A relative? A friend? Someone who owed
him? Whoever it is, they worry. They hesitate to take such a
risk. Surveillance has increased since the start of the summer.
The police force assigned to the "Jewish question" sets traps
in the tunnels of the metro, at the exits of cinemas and theaters, in public parks. With the bright fabric on his chest, he
could be picked up anywhere. Coming home, a line appears,
people gather, and suddenly there's a roadblock in the distance,
a checkpoint, men in uniforms inspecting papers, orders flying
through the air. If he turns around, he'll be picked up immediately. So he edges away, very slowly, imperceptibly. There's no
reverse gear on a quadricycle. The only way to go backward is
to put your feet on the ground and push the machine toward
you. His handicapped passenger watches him sweat, tense his
muscles, grip the handlebars. The soles of his shoes skid; the
wheels scrape the asphalt. The bike chain turns without the
pedals. Up ahead, the crowd that was concealing them begins
to break up. If they leave too much space between themselves
and the cars in front, they risk attracting the attention of the
police or the soldiers. As the last pedestrians and vehicles are
about to reach the barricade, he sees an escape. He inches back

another meter or two, readies his Vélocar, and disappears down a side street.

16

This time, he walks alone. In the middle of the night, he goes down the kitchen stairs and heads to the street with his overcoat, his hat, and a little suitcase. Defying the German ordinance that forbids him to leave his place of residence between the hours of eight at night and six in the morning. Was it the end of summer or already the fall of 1942? He'd stopped seeing his patients. The Public Welfare Supervisory Board of the City of Paris is about to declare his post vacant. He is officially divorced from his spouse. His bank account is frozen. There's nothing left to keep him in Paris. With a determined step, he crosses the courtyard, reaches the entryway, lifts the latch, and pulls the door toward him, slamming it hard, as if he wanted the whole world—family, concierge, neighbors, local residents, police informants, and passing strangers—to hear it.

Kitchen

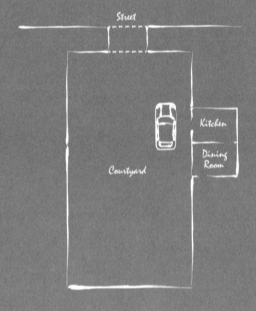

Street

Courtyard

Kitchen

Dining
Room

1

There was a time when a property was distinguished by the number and quality of its locks. Inside a bourgeois house, everything was kept carefully shut: doors, wardrobes, desks, cubbies, drawers, cellars, attics. It was actually considered the sign of a good household. The wealth and the respectability of a place were measured by the rattle of its key ring. Nothing was owned that couldn't be latched, padlocked, stuffed away. Everyone eventually has the experience of cleaning out an apartment after a death, collecting keys with unknown uses. Keys of all sizes—big, gilded, coppery, rust colored, gray, stunted, thick, tubular, with circular pins or notches. Keys cloaked in mystery, which often lead nowhere, orphan keys kept out of doubt or nostalgia, protecting things you can only guess at, concealing wealth, treasure chests, gardens, vegetable patches, garages, entire fortunes made manifest yet invisible.

For a long time, Rue-de-Grenelle had only one key—flat, notched, triangular, not heavy, lost and copied a thousand times—which opened everything. It unlocked—and still unlocks—an old creaking double door with two glass panels and a handle on each side. The kind that, even if you forgot your set of keys upstairs, wouldn't keep you locked out. For years, the right side has banged the tile floor. Its wood has swelled, the hinges have sagged. To open it, you have to turn the knob and, if possible, lift it slightly, pressing a little harder each day with your foot on the warped bottom of the door. Once you cross the threshold, you arrive in the kitchen, a room much-darkened by the aluminum venetian blinds that cover the two lower glass panels with twisted slats that block the light. To reach her car, mère-grand always used these doors. We did the same. Strangers who came to the house went through the two other, more formal entrances at the end of the garden: guests passed through the foyer, while patients, students, or employees were channeled through the little parlor.

The different entrances created a functional division of the house, keeping private rooms separate from professional or social space. Each part had its own door. The kitchen was never locked until the seventies, when a painting of a sheep in a pasture by the sea disappeared. Followed, a few months later, by a black marble clock. After these two thefts, which were never explained, we started to bolt it. A purely symbolic measure. If the burglar wanted to commit another crime, he would only have to push one of the unlocked ground-floor windows. Things weren't important. Only people. And no lock, no surveillance camera, no intercom could protect them from the dangers that threatened, whether they were real or imagined. For protection, they relied on their unshakable unity, a tie stronger than any security chain. And so the Rue-de-Grenelle was a microcosm, at once open and self-sufficient. We weren't shut-ins, but we stuck together.

2

The kitchen could be called square if it followed straight lines. The fixtures it needed to function, which had once been hidden behind coverings, slats, and casings, were now exposed, like in some modern architecture. It was a hodgepodge of piping, cables, meters, gauges. The furnishings consisted of a few cupboards that had been there for at least a half century, with peeling countertops redone in imitation oak Formica. Little scattered carrot-colored tiles, flecked with plaster and grease, adorned a water main that ran more or less parallel to the doorway, emphasizing its off-kilter lines. The tiles also sprinkled the upper half of the left-hand wall reserved for the appliances. This orange mosaic enshrined a stainless-steel sink, an old gas stove, and a dishwasher, which, after a long life of energy guzzling, was mainly used as a dish dryer because of calcium deposits and crystallized food scraps. A yellowed, food-splattered paint job covered the other three sides of the room and the ceiling.

Though the wall decorations evolved with time, their themes didn't change. The little etching of a mail coach that hung over the faucet was a reminder of other English stage coaches that had once decorated the adjacent dining room. My grandfather used the pictures as a canvas, a visual aid for the stories he invented to entertain the children, gathering them in his arms and hoisting them up to the frame. On the back right side, a reproduction watercolor of the three-masted ship *Saint-Vincent-de-Paul* echoed other nautical paintings that had also vanished. It was done by Antoine Roux, the painter from Marseille. A large-format print of a pair of sprouting potatoes hung on that same right wall in place of another photo of a steak with *frites* and a glass of wine against a monochrome mauve backdrop— one of Christian's early works dating from the seventies, when he was trying out variations on the classic still life. These images referring to other, more ancient ones, this self-referencing, these mirrors within mirrors only perceptible to the initiated are typical of a system turned in on itself.

If a house can be compared to a palimpsest, to a tablet you erase to write on again, then the Rue-de-Grenelle would look, to all outsiders, like an illegible scribble. Only the most familiar with it could spot in all the clutter the inevitable changes over the years. Usually in consultation with his sister Anne, Jean-Élie undertook tiny rearrangements, little erasures, minute additions. Like the Ramadan lamp and blown-glass globes from Egypt that appeared on the white laminated sideboard, or the enameled biscuit tin on the kitchen table, refilled only with Petit Brun butter cookies, which joined a chipped crystal salt shaker and the ebony case that used to sit on my grandfather's desk, full of papers for the car. For most people, these alterations were invisible, but for me, attentive as I am to the tiniest ruptures in this timeless place, they hold a considerable importance.

3

After his parents died, Jean-Élie moved downstairs as if he were withdrawing into a tomb. He kept the apartment as it was. He simply retreated, made room, gave away a few pieces of furniture and moved others without changing the general arrangement. "Below," as we call it, hasn't become a museum so much as an intimate temple, and he is the guardian. His respect for the space is less a desire to mull over the past or a taste for relics than an asceticism, a letting things go, an indifference to material possessions. For the sake of convenience, he eats his meals in the kitchen and uses the old dining area as a storeroom. This second space, transformed into an extension of the first—hence its presence in this chapter—consists of a sofa bed where I occasionally sleep, a chair upholstered in marigold-colored velvet, a side table, a long, narrow bench, moving boxes that have never been emptied, coats hanging on a three-hook rack fixed to the back of the door, a dish cabinet turned into a bookcase displaying volumes piled or arranged in rows, and a backgammon table inlaid with ivory where a few knickknacks rest that had once been on view in the living room.

A mother-of-pearl set of opera glasses, a tissue paper flower, a crystal vase, an indigo Chinese teapot, a baccarat paperweight shaped like a fish, a chain-mail purse from 1900 adorned with a gold metal clasp. I don't know if any of these objects has sentimental value for him.

For as long as I can remember, he has dressed the same way. He wears a faded pair of Levi's 501s, a shirt with thin stripes, a blue sweater, usually thrown over his shoulders, and black leather boots. For lunch, if he's alone, he always has a glass of red wine and a piece of bread with an egg in a bed of harissa, which he gets from a Cap Bon tube with a simple squeeze of the thumb. After clearing the table and drinking a cup of leftover morning coffee, reheated in a little pot, he thoughtfully smokes a cigarillo, gazing out the window. He must be one of the beings I love most in this world, but he's always remained a mystery. I'm unable to guess when he's sad, happy, calm, worried, or frustrated. He never complains. His voice is always soft and measured. I've only rarely seen him angry, and never violent. Once in a while he'll groan and bare his teeth, like a cat—usually when someone tries to refuse his help. He is affectionate, considerate, there for us all, but he doesn't confide in us. Or very rarely.

Though he has carefully read, if not partly rewritten, all the manuscripts produced by his family, he never mentions his own intellectual work. In a bookstore, we stumble by accident on learned works about language, phonology, the Chomskyan revolution, that he'd written and published months or years earlier without ever letting us know. His encyclopedic knowledge encompasses Latin and Greek antiquity with a particular taste for the late Roman empire, quattrocento painting, the French Revolution, English literature from Geoffrey Chaucer

to Virginia Woolf, international cinema, linguistics (which is
his field), as well as developments in macroeconomics, medicine, epistemology, Chinese philosophy, and on and on. He
can speak for hours on the obscure origins of the Etruscan language, Watson and Crick's discovery of the double helix, the de-
ciphering of Linear B by the British architect Michael Ventris,
the great London plague of 1665, the bizarre life of the poet
William Blake, director Fritz Lang's struggle with the Nazis,
or even the night a young Alfred Hitchcock spent at a police
station and the effects of this traumatic experience on his films.
From a daily reading of *Le Monde* and an almost hypermnesic
memory, he's able to recount the smallest events from the news
of these last seventy years. But he has never said much about
himself, about us.

If someone asks him how he is, he'll say "fine" in a tone that
discourages any further questions. When I finally dared to tell
him I was writing a book about the Rue-de-Grenelle, he told
me, enunciating each word, that it was a "good idea." Then he
changed the subject. I waited a few more weeks before asking
him if I could pose a few questions. I was afraid of sadden-
ing him by forcing him to plunge back into what was clearly a
pretty mortifying past. He must have noticed my embarrassment. On the phone, though I thought I heard a slight hesitation in his voice, he agreed as usual. I came over for lunch
on a weekday. He had bought tinned pâté and opened a can of
green peas. My stomach was in knots for the whole meal. He
answered my questions without any departure from his usual
calm good humor. During each interview, we stood side by side
in the kitchen. He smoked, his back pressed to the sideboard.
I stood by the door with my notebook. On the threshold of my
subject. Like a visitor to someone's pantry, not knowing if he's
welcome, hesitates to leave or explore the other rooms.

4

The first thing I did whenever I came home from school, before even taking off my coat, was to open the fridge. I stuck my head inside, drooling, searching for something to nibble on. Usually I didn't find anything besides ground coffee, a tub of margarine, a bottle of Worcestershire sauce, a box of crackers, a jar of dried-up pickles, the rolled-up tube of harissa noted above, and a few eggs tucked away in their compartments on the refrigerator door. Sometimes, in the crisper, next to a wilted head of lettuce, I'd find a hidden packet of smoked ham in wax paper and gobble it down immediately. I dug through every cranny of the bread box too, in search of hypothetical pastries. I gulped stale cookies, gnawed dry chunks of bread, and emptied the bottoms of jam jars. I was hungry. I wasn't the only one to rummage that hopelessly empty larder. To this day, when the kitchen door's creaks give way to the refrigerator's opening squeal, my uncle Christian has announced his arrival.

To put it plainly, at the Rue-de-Grenelle there was nothing to eat. Mère-grand, who was afraid of gaining weight and being unable to hoist herself up if her body became too heavy, pecked at crumbs like a bird. She might have weighed seventy pounds. The weight of a child. In a spirit of solidarity, Jean-Élie and Anne mimicked her, subjecting themselves to the same weight-loss regimen. Only grand-papa, always served first, had a right to a more substantial portion, as if he were still growing. At restaurants, to watch their figures (and to save money) they ordered a succession of appetizers and side dishes. The waiter, after writing down an order of fries, a deviled egg, mixed vegetables, a celery remoulade, would inevitably ask, "and for the main course?" The four of them ate like one person. Once,

when they entered a fancy, prix-fixe restaurant by accident
and hesitated to get up from the table, they ordered one single
three-course menu, the cheapest, which they divided up as each
course arrived, saving the biggest helpings for grand-papa.
Even when they fed themselves, they formed only one body.

5

Their house was a palace, and they lived like hobos. It would
be wrong to chalk up this vagabond mixture of scarcity, dirt,
and stinginess to some upper-class eccentricity. Their bizarro
behavior was a rejection of good manners and social conventions. It declared a rebellion against their peers. It also created
an insider's club, a break with the outside world, and was in
this sense somewhat pathological. The usual hierarchy was
overrun. Luxury mixed with want. My grandfather once reproached himself for the death of a cancer patient, thinking he
hadn't caught it in time. Ever since, for mysterious reasons that
prompted endless family jokes, her tycoon husband sent a case
of champagne each year. The best. They drank the priceless
bottles as if they were the usual rotgut, without the least bit of
ceremony, as they ate their scraps. They didn't eat lunch—they
picnicked. They grabbed food on the run. Every meal was a
stopgap. The house hadn't always been this way. Up until the
middle of the sixties, while a little of its grandeur remained,
a maid in uniform, believe it or not, did the cleaning and the
cooking. A Breton woman called Berthe, and then Amalia,
who was Spanish. As in other bourgeois interiors, the lady of
the house rang a little silver bell when the dishes should be
cleared.

6

I wasn't underfed. Since I gobbled everything that came my way, I actually became a rather chubby kid. Wisely, I didn't wait for the pittance to arrive on my plate. I took advance measures. I stole from the source, from the pot on the stove. By adopting the neighborhood etiquette, my mother always left the Rue-de-Grenelle with an empty stomach. While she waited politely to be served, her knife and fork placed on either side of her plate, everyone else threw themselves at the food in a joyful melee. The lunches that took place in the dining room, under a crystal chandelier, were moments of glee, freedom, confusion. Guests might turn up at any moment. No one asked whether there was enough food for everyone. I once heard Jean-Élie tell a dozen companions, "What luck! I bought three chocolate éclairs." There were no table manners. We could eat with our hands, kneel on the bench, plunge our forks into the serving dish, lick the plates, wipe our hands on our clothes. Christian claims that his father used to tell him to run his greasy fingers through his hair to fortify it. But I never personally heard him say that.

In this enclosed universe, we ate a lot of canned food. Mont Blanc desert puddings—vanilla, chocolate, or Grand-Marnier. Precooked Garbit couscous with meat. Sometimes a whole assortment of these tins. Ready-made food. Buitoni ravioli with (and this was Jean-Élie's personal touch) a bit of condensed milk. Beans that he heated up in tomato sauce in an attempt to make baked beans à l'anglaise. These canned delicacies were judged by only one criteria: whether or not they were safe to eat. The contents had to be sterile and tightly sealed. At the slightest swelling of the lid, the slightest opening whistle, they ended up in the trash.

7

We were afraid. Of everything, of nothing, of others, of ourselves. Of spoiled food. Of rotten eggs. Of crowds and their prejudices, their hatreds, their longings. Of sickness as well as the ways to combat it. Of the pill you take after obsessively reading Vidal's medical dictionary. Of asphyxiating from a gas leak. Of drowning at sea, of avalanches in the mountains. Of cars. Of accidents. Of people in uniform. Of anyone vested with some sort of power, and therefore a power to harm. Of official forms. Of bureaucratic processes. Of little stories and major history. Of false happiness. Of the light, which implies the dark. Of honest people who, depending on the circumstances, can transform into criminals. Of the French who define themselves as good in opposition to those they judge as bad. Of gossipy neighbors. Of human fickleness, and of life's reversals. Of the worst, since it's sure to happen.

Very early, almost at birth, I inherited this dread from my family. As a toddler, I was afraid of hot sand, waves, wild mushrooms, tall grass, trees rubbing against each other, shadows, sweet old women whom I mistook for witches, spiders, and, more generally, any kind of insect. I was an anxious child. In restaurants, to make me behave, my parents would point out one or two old people in the room, preferably wrinkled and oozing. I would stop crying at once for fear that they would turn me into a frog. On vacation, as a way of getting a break, they would put me in the middle of the beach towel, on the sand or the lawn. In the midst of those inhospitable wilds, I would stay put until they returned, without daring to step off the fabric.

As I got older, my terrors grew to include flying saucers, nights with a full moon, dark corners, open wardrobes, and dogs, whether they were leashed or not.

My father lived in fear of nuclear holocaust. He knew pretty much everything about the Manhattan Project. During the Cold War, he predicted the end of the world every time tensions between the United States and the Soviet Union increased. Ever since, his nights remain haunted by visions of "strange spaceships, advancing toward the unknown." As a teenager, Christian was already painting endless scenes of war that fell somewhere between *Guernica* and *The Blue Circus*, between the nightmares of Picasso and the dreams of Chagall. His frescoes of oriental icons pouring the blood of Christ were coated in a cooking-oil-based paint he'd concocted himself, which until recently left a slight stain whenever anyone brushed up against the canvas. One particularly beautiful and frightening example covered one of the walls in the old dining room with a chaos of burning airplanes, rubble, and terrified humans. Jean-Élie would shout at us to "be careful"—an interjection he usually repeated twice—before undertakings as basic as crossing the street or turning on the faucet.

As for their mother, she controlled every instant of their lives. After they reached adulthood and acquired their dearly bought autonomy, she ordered that they keep her informed of their movements. If they were a few minutes late with a call or a meeting, she imagined horrifying disasters. One evening, I heard her call the station to ask if the train carrying one of her sons had derailed.

8

The twelve tolls of Big Ben rang through the upstairs and provided our lunchtime bell. After the war, my grandfather never

missed the BBC news broadcast in French, which went out
at noon (London time) every day, on AM radio. He never listened to any other channel. He pressed his little transistor to
his ear with a feverish hand, probably out of worry that the
transmission would be garbled. The retractable antenna was
always stretched out horizontally for greater privacy as he listened for the liberating bells of Westminster. The news, which
was slightly removed from French current events, was read in a
clear, slow voice, with a cadence that marked each pause. This
style, which was typical of broadcasting from the United King-
dom, had a hint of foreignness. He followed the news with a
nervous air, as if he were holding a clandestine transmitter and
feared the German radio intercept trucks would find him. As
soon as the program ended, he came to the table.

9

When she wanted to please, she went down to the kitchen early
in the morning and got to work at the stove. On her wobbling
feet, buttressed by the buffet, she cored and stuffed peppers,
grilled eggplant on the gas range, cutting their charred skins
off with a knife and mixing their flesh with caramelized onions.
She salted cucumbers, then plunged them into heavy cream.
She kneaded the meatballs, rolled them in egg and then in
breadcrumbs, tossed them in boiling oil, then dusted them with
paprika. She cut and sautéed chicken livers. The kitchen filled
with smells of garlic, charred eggplant, frying. Its walls reso-
nated with sounds of chopping and with bizarre names: kacha,
vareniki, pojarski, vatrouchka. On special occasions, and generally Sundays, she made borscht. A soup of beets, cabbage,
and brisket that she let simmer the previous day, before skim-
ming off the grease and serving it with pierogies and knishes

from Goldenberg's. As a final touch, she added powdered sugar and a finger of vinegar, measuring out each ingredient with the precision of a lab technician. The secret of borscht lies in a very precarious balance between sweet and sour.

To celebrate, she got out the nicest china, a blue porcelain. The bowls for soup and the plates for the meat. She offered us not so much a feast as a past. She communicated a history that wasn't hers, sacrificing to an ancient cult whose rites she had adopted. She performed a kind of Eucharist. Her hearty soup, slightly tart and smelling of cabbage, contained the transubstantiation of the Boltanskis' soul. In three to four spoonfuls of magic potion, she gave us origins, a feeling of belonging if not to a community then at least to a culinary model, something that allowed us to reclaim, or better yet, justify our difference. Images rose out of her cauldrons—steppes, sleds gliding over the snow, sacred chants, Shabbat candles, a bewitched gypsy orchestra. She, who ate nothing, bequeathed this traditional cuisine as a final settlement. No exotic folklore, no ancestral dress to respect, no rare language to save from oblivion, no cultural inheritance to bring across new borders. Only recipes. Food she called "Russian" so as not to say "Jewish."

She didn't do all this for us, but for him. Her offerings were destined only for her husband. The borscht, the Pojarski cutlets, filled an absence, like the pastrami or the strudel we bought in the Marais. They allowed her to put words (or really dishes) to what was always there but never spoken. He didn't ask for anything. He didn't say anything. She was the only one to break the silence, to dare to pronounce an adjective he had tried to eradicate. She dragged him to the Pletzel on Sunday mornings. She re-created the flavors of Odessa. Left to his own devices, he would have preferred to remain anonymous and settle for some Breton specialties, which she might have learned if her own family had been interested in gastronomy or in raising her as their child. When she joined him in a marriage that took her away from her people, she married everything: what he was and what he no longer wished to be. She cooked up dishes from his childhood to reconcile him with himself, to give him back a sense of pride, an equilibrium, a seat at the table.

10

She was initiated into this Eastern-European cuisine by her mother-in-law. A woman who died four years before I was born, who shared the housekeeping and lived upstairs. The family remembers this chimeric person by the affectionate term Niania, which could be translated as *nounou* or *mémé*. She was never referred to by anything other than this nickname, straight out of a Russian novel, as if, for her whole life, she'd been nothing but this: an old nurse overcome with love for her children. I don't know what she looked like. I have no family album to search through, no sepia-colored portrait preserved in a wooden frame. Photos are forbidden in the Rue-de-Grenelle because they show what no longer exists. The little I know of Niania I got from my father and my uncles.

She was, apparently, a short woman, full figured, with long brown hair. Always dressed in black, as if she were condemned to an eternal widowhood. Christian depicts her in a babushka with her hair dyed, wearing a vest embroidered with flowers, permanently troubled by rheumatism, a woman who would say "Eem cahhming!" whenever anyone called for her. At the end of the day, they listened to Russian music on her gramophone. Especially a record of songs from the Volga, which he found a copy of years later in Brancusi's studio when it was reconstructed at the Centre Pompidou. He claims she had a strong Yiddish accent. Jean-Élie says the opposite—that she pronounced French correctly but couldn't write. Luc never heard her play music, and he assured me she never had a gramophone. He mostly remembers grilled eggplant sandwiches, and her habit, when she came to babysit him, of always arriving an hour early, with a book by the Countess de Ségur and a candle in case of a power outage. In her nasal voice and her rolled *r*'s she read him *General Dourakine* and told him his father would become a cabinet minister. She was equally passionate about her only son and about France, the country that had welcomed her.

11

All I know of Niania is her samovar. A symbolic object that embodied the myth of the tribe. The totem of the Boltanskis. In my memory, it was once displayed in the dining room cupboard. After its disappearance, I had confused it for a long time with the leather base of a lamp that was given pride of place at my mother's and that now lights my bedroom, though pretty weakly. In fact, Christian restored the samovar after his parents died. He had been tempted to sell it to a collector, like an artwork, and seized with remorse, forged the man a copy. At least that's what he claims. The samovar served as cover image for my grandmother's last book, dedicated to her spouse and his long suffering in the intensive care unit. In the black-and-white photograph on the front of a little book called *Resucideception*, the samovar looks daintier and less vivid than the Russian portable kettles in the windows of antique stores. It was never used, to my knowledge, at least not after its transformation into a statue. As opposed to the totem pole, which for Freud is a representation of the father, this was all about feminine roundness, a protruding belly, two coiled handles,

and a scalloped base to accommodate the kettle. Or at least it
was androgynous, with its tiny spout no longer spilling forth
any liquid. A source of heat, a tool for sharing, it symbolized the
hearth, and therefore the household, the group, the ancestor,
but also the uprooting, the forgotten country, those who had
been left behind. A shedding of skin.

Our emblem was the result of a theft. Niania was running
away from home when she took this samovar, which must have
still been boiling hot. Why did she encumber herself with an
ordinary object, something every Russian family possessed?
To remember, most likely, the family she was leaving and to
prepare for the one she would establish. To create a common
thread between her two dissimilar lives. Before she fled, she
wrote to her father, a merchant who imported cattle and grapes
from Corinth. A wealthy man who owned a sleigh with bells.
Later, this detail would become central to the stories she told.
This jingling cord hooked to the harness was the definitive sign,
the thing that proved her high rank in society. In her letter,
she told him she planned to join David, her lover. An opera
singer whose triumphant career had been brutally interrupted
by illness. And worse, he was a lowborn young man, someone
her parents wouldn't have wanted in the family, from a class
that was too poor and too religious. In their eyes, not Russian
enough: his artisan father feared the Almighty, still wore the
black brimmed hat and ritual tassels, and didn't let *goyim* into
his house. But where her lover had gone, these details were no
longer important. He lived in a fabulous land, the first to have
liberated the Jews—before long he would be rich and happy.
She ended the letter with an ode to France. Together, they
would begin a new life in this generous, welcoming country,
where all citizens, no matter their origins or beliefs, were free
and equal.

Apparently she hadn't reached the age of legal adulthood. She changed the date of birth on her passport to be able to travel. With her falsified papers, she feared she'd be detained each time she crossed a border. Her samovar was too wide to fit in a suitcase—she must have had it under her arm when she got off the train in Paris. David was waiting for her on the platform. He'd forgotten how young she was. She didn't recognize him right away either. A year earlier, she'd said goodbye to an artist. I imagine him looking like Aristide Bruant as Toulouse Lautrec sketched him, or at least with the same stature: a hat with a wide brim, a black coat, and a red scarf wrapped around his throat. This time she found a laborer in work overalls, thinner, a prematurely aged face. After making her climb six flights of stairs in a tenement building and settling her in his tiny room under the eaves, he told her he had to go work. He was on the night shift. That night and the following nights she was left alone in this garret, which was unfurnished apart from a cot, a chair, and a trunk covered with Cyrillic characters. She considered going back to Odessa and throwing herself at her father's feet, to implore his mercy and give him back his samovar. But she was a prisoner of her letter, her lyricism, and above all, her pride as she described her country of adoption and her future happiness. Jean-Élie admits, with his usual tact that "she was a bit disappointed." But after all, he adds, she and her husband made "a very good household."

12

I'm aware that all of this flows from a single source: Niania, whose life accustomed her to disguising, sweetening, magnifying. Over almost a century, this story must have been told dozens of times by a limited number of people—five or six at most.

With time, it acquired the force of legend, a fable with its faults taken out, smoothed by years of manipulation. It hardened, like modeling paste. It ended up drying out and then becoming brittle. I hurry to get it on paper before it crumbles and is lost forever. There is, of course, some element of truth to it. The story grew from pieces of memory and, once upon a time, real events. Each person I interviewed told a slightly different version. This series of alterations has its own logic and gives these tiny details a shine, a depth, a weight. They tell their own story of exile, of an immigrant required, like so many others, to lie for her survival, of her descendants struggling to understand, and finally of time passing, of oblivion.

13

Nothing changes. The family continues to eat their meals at the long, extendable table. Each person sits in the same place around the olive-green waxed tablecloth. Jean-Élie and Anne on the bench, which matches the one by the lighted stove in the adjoining room. They leave the cinema seats, leaning back against the wall, to the others—the only new addition, a fantasy that would have been unfathomable in their mother's time. Too unstable. Upholstered in velvet the color of wine dregs, the folding seats lurch dangerously as soon as you sit down because the metal bar that connects them isn't attached to the floor. She couldn't have supported herself on them. Not without risking a fall. The furniture served as her crutches, her guardrails, her buttresses and armrests. It sketched an invisible path across the house, like carabiner hooks left for mountain climbers on a rocky slope. Without her, the pieces became useless, only good for draping with shrouds. She breathed life into them. Her rage, her energy still radiates from the walls. You can almost see her swinging between the table and the sideboard, her hands gripping the wicker chair she pushed in front of her instead of a walker, her features straining, almost grimacing with anger and restrained violence as if she fought a bloody battle with herself and everything around her. We were attentive to her smallest gesture, ready to rush to her aid, and all the while holding back, at a respectful distance, looking up so as not to meet her gaze, since she only recognized her difference in the eyes of others. In the evenings, when we're together in the kitchen, we keep looking away. We don't talk about her or about him. We never bring up our memories of them, not by omission or indifference but out of discretion. As if they were still there.

14

After "Monsieur's" flight, the concierge becomes even more intrusive than usual. She barges in all the time, her little girl at her heels, to offer her help, to announce a shipment of vegetables at some grocer or other, or to tell the latest neighborhood gossip. She tries to make herself useful, probably moved by this handicapped woman who by all appearances was raising two boys on her own. She must have been shocked by the behavior of this husband who just went and abandoned his family in the middle of a war, and she said as much to other residents of the building. From the kitchen, right across from her door, they hear her every word. Her "Fine, go away!" and her "What are you looking at? Don't you have something better to do?" echo through the courtyard like her wireless, which endlessly broadcasts speeches by Pétain and Laval. Can they trust her? Is she collaborating with the authorities like other superintendents? She's at least as entranced by Philippe Henriot as the old spinster dressmaker who comes to the house, and Henriot, in his role as an editorialist for Radio Paris, was nicknamed "the French Goebbels." She complains about the "Boches" and sometimes lets slip critical opinions about the "Maréchal." But if she suspected anything, she could tell someone, so she's dangerous. At the end of 1942 a bell was added by the kitchen door to signal her intrusions.

15

I move across the Rue-de-Grenelle like the board in a game of Clue. By a lucky coincidence, there are as many pawns as protagonists. Besides Colonel Mustard, it's easy to choose who would be Miss Scarlett, Mrs. Peacock, Professor Plum, Mr. Green, or Mrs. White. I don't need to throw the dice. In fact, I can progress in only one direction, only one room at a time, or two if they perform the same function, like the kitchen and the former dining room. The series of connected rooms have economical hallways and nowhere to escape—which is really their drawback. With each turn, I discover a new room. Unlike the classic version of the game, there's no secret passage linking the office to the observatory (in our case the terrace) or the bathroom to the parlor. I never encountered a club, either, or a dagger, or a revolver. Instead of clues, I place a key here, a half-empty fridge there, a samovar, and a bell. In each piece of the house, I invoke one or more characters, I test each alibi, I offer a hypothesis, and I get closer and closer to the truth. If the victim is the same as in Clue, the mystery isn't. I'm not at the scene of a murder but of a disappearance. That's the question I need to answer—where is the doctor hiding?

Office

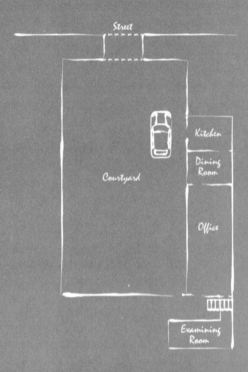

Street

Courtyard

Kitchen

Dining Room

Office

Examining Room

1

For a long time, he continued to appear in the phone book as a specialist in gastroenterology. His telephone, a gray plastic model from the late sixties with a rotary dial, was balanced on the office mantel, facing a gilt mirror. It rang frequently, especially during business hours. As soon as I picked up, I'd hear someone's irritable or diuretic voice on the other end of the line, which sounded to me like the other side of the grave. These desperate calls demanding urgent appointments had a glacial effect on me. A few times I was tempted to do what these unfortunate people wanted so that I could provide them with something even better than care—the few comforting words he was so good at providing. If not for his reflection, which I kept expecting to see in the mirror, his walker, his treatises, his reference books crowded on the shelves, if not for all the gravity I, as a child, associated with his lifesaving mission—his lofty research, his magnum opus—I would probably have received them, wrapped in a white coat to be more credible, a costume he never bothered with. "The doctor is no longer practicing," Jean-Élie would reply, in a measured tone, always in the present tense. He waited two decades before changing the France Télécom account and putting it in his own name.

2

In this drowsy office, my uncle erases any trace of himself. He sleeps on the couch where his father took a quick nap after lunch. Once he gets up, he tucks his sheets, his pillowcase, and his tartan blanket into the cavity of a cherry dresser. He works

at a Directoire-style table covered in crushed velvet and lit by
a mother-of-pearl lamp in the shape of a mushroom, which
emphasizes the darkness of the room rather than brightening
it. No sooner has he closed his books and folders than he stows
them away in cubbies or drawers. No underwear forgotten in a
corner, no papers thrown in the wastebasket, no sweater hung
on the back of a chair. He doesn't leave anything lying around:
not personal effects, not mail addressed to him. Like a stow-
away in his own house, he makes the slightest signs of his life
disappear over the course of the day. In winter, I find him sitting on the iron radiator, turned toward the last window in a
row of three, or if not there, sitting on the floor in front of a pale
wooden side table or a little octagonal stand, back pressed to
his bed, his boots glued to a space heater, folded in on himself,
as if he wanted to take up the least space possible lest his presence fill the whole house.

He also likes to spend his evenings huddled in one of his
mail-order rocking chairs, of mediocre quality so that they often need replacing. He watches the Mezzo channel for classical
music and jazz, but he leaves the sound off. He likes to watch
the silent movements of fingers on the keyboards, the equally
noiseless staccato sawings of bows, the conductor's mechanical
gestures, like a toy robot whose spring needs to be wound, the
desperate efforts of soundless divas, the tenors who, deprived
of their voices, seem to cry for help with waving arms and wide-
open mouths, all these chests that fill and exhale in the same
rhythm like punctured bagpipes making no sound, musicians
bent over white sheets of music that seem to call for nothing
but a litany of rests, half rests, and sighs. Muzzled, reduced to
a series of fixed movements, the opera is nothing but a stiff,
grotesque pantomime, a heavy machinery that churns emptily
on. These mute images, deprived of all but visual interest, these

thousands of pixels left to themselves, make the silence in the office grow heavier. This is Jean-Élie's omertà.

3

When he's alone, he keeps the chandelier turned off. He only lights it on grand occasions, when he has visitors. The rest of the time, he likes the twilight of lampshades, better suited to a space that he uses as both a bedroom and a place to visit. The harsh light hanging in the center of the room brings out the peeling paint, the scratched walls, the chips in the old herringbone parquet—and most notably the hole by the dining room door, which someone put a chair over to prevent anybody falling in. With its copper branches, its blackened glass, its candles halfway burned down, this lighting bears witness to past splendors and latter-day decline. It belongs to another era, another category. Too big, too low. It's oversized, given the height of the ceiling, and must have been intended for Lilliputians. People bump their heads on the ornaments hanging from the chandelier on wrought iron chains; the crystals sway into each other with a ringing sound and eventually fall one by one, like overripe fruit.

It's crazy what lighting, even faded, will do: just one flip of a switch and the office comes back to life. A long room, wallpapered in bottle green. Like the other rooms at the Rue-de-Grenelle, this one kept its habitual title. We continue to call it the "office," despite its living-room furnishings, and more importantly, the absence of a desk—that one-syllable word which would give it a reason for being. But the desk is missing. A handsome Louis XIII table, varnished, with carved legs ending in wooden balls. Basically the only thing my father kept. He wrote most of his essays, his plays, his poems on its thick wooden planks. An object that has traveled quite a bit but remains tied to one place and one place only. Taken out of its original environment, I barely recognize it. It's become strange to me. But I remember the exact spot it occupied, in the back, at the center of the room. It was bracketed by two cabinets, almost touching the shutters of the French windows. It had a built-in writing case covered in black leather that held white letterhead and blank prescriptions. I still make a detour to avoid its four steel corners, like a mutilated person still feels a phantom limb, a part that's no longer attached, but its absence can be haunting and painful. It marks a space with invisible frontiers; it leaves an emptiness, but a full one, containing hundreds of fleeting images. In its place a low, narrow table, elongated almost like a bench, its pale, pine surface stained with rings from glasses, vainly tries to make us forget.

4

The chair is still there. It appears in a ten-minute film directed by my grandmother and the poet Raphaël Cluzel in 1984. Filmed from behind and close-up, this mustard yellow armchair, stocky, with padded armrests, actually had the starring role. Standing on either side of the chair, a husband—played by a professional actor—and his wife—played by my mother, who was performing her second and last on-screen part—debate the health of an indeterminate person resting on the seat, whom they suppose to be asleep. The couple is going on vacation and discusses, with an embarrassment bordering on compassion, what they should do with this burden, who could just as easily be a feeble old man or a household pet. My older sister, Ariane, is there too, in the role of sulky teenager.

The film explores the contrast back then between a public

outcry about the dogs left along French highways after everybody went away for summer vacation and a general indifference
toward old people, abandoned during the summer months and
neglected for the rest of the year. For us, this fable had a particular meaning, both sarcastic and sad. That chair was his. That's
where he liked to smoke his pipe, where he flipped through
his medical journals in the evenings, where he told me stories,
where he burst into tears after reading a passage from Dickens
or Dostoyevsky or Victor Hugo. Where he was no longer.

During the filming, did she imagine him sitting against the
oval, upholstered back? Was she looking for him through that
tall camera, taller than she was? Did she hope to find some
trace of him on the film itself, like those believers in UFOs who
snap pictures of the sky, looking for the slightest optical dis-
turbance? Did she want to capture him in her darkroom? For
the purposes of the movie, the suite had been converted into a
cinema studio. An editing table borrowed by the producer had
appeared in what was once the examining room, a windowless
space, smelling of soap and ether, which was connected to the
office by a narrow corridor. The steel panel weighed a ton. It
was pushed against the wall next to a rudimentary X-ray machine, an examining table, and a medicine cabinet. It could almost have passed for another piece of medical equipment with
its trays, its arrays of buttons, its frame counters, and its little
portal for viewing. Already antique, it stayed there for years,
abandoned, until the space became a bathroom, with a toilet
alcove and small tub.

5

I stood up straight, shirtless, while he laid out his instruments
on a metal box with wheels. When he needed to give me a shot,

his hand trembled. He was afraid of hurting me and hesitated over the angle of attack, bumping the syringe and having to start over, prolonging the pain of the needle in spite of himself. I remember how much it bothered him to strike my tibia or my kneecap with his leather mallet, his anxious voice asking me to cough or hold my breath, his cautious fingers finding their way between my shoulder blades, coming back around, going over my goose-bumped skin. It must have hurt him to inflict pain, to stick in a needle or track some anomaly with his stethoscope. He wasn't a bad doctor. Quite the opposite—he was extremely careful. Too careful, even. His checkups were endless. Afraid he would make some diagnostic error, he listened to my chest with such minute care, such infinite slowness, but also with reticence, begrudgingly, as if every time he feared the worst. He was just as terrified of missing something as of finding it. He didn't like his job.

He was incapable of treating an open wound. He couldn't handle the sight of blood. He couldn't go into a butcher shop or eat rare meat without nearly fainting. One evening, at a fancy dinner party, he turned pale at the sight of a steak dripping hemoglobin. He tried to make it disappear under the table, but was caught by the hostess, who burst out laughing. With the tips of his fingers, he sheepishly pulled the lump out of his napkin and put it back on his plate with a disgusted air, as if he'd found a dead rat. He was equally horrified by organ meats: sweetbreads, brain, tripe, feet, ears. The carnal part of his profession, that confrontation with suffering bodies, all those epiglottises to inspect, those lymph nodes to palpitate, gargles to listen to, pulses to take, bacteria to fight, all this was revolting. Life's simmering frightened him. Death was even worse. He couldn't stand it. Losing a patient left him deeply depressed. He preferred theory to practice. His books. His research. The antiseptic whiteness of labs. Without illusions. He knew the limits of science. Convinced that his chosen enemy preyed on the mechanisms of the body as much as the forces of the spirit, he liked to explore areas that his peers ignored—like the unconscious, madness, psychosomatic symptoms. He would have made an excellent analyst.

He never put a doctor's symbol on the dashboard of his car. He didn't see the point of hanging a tarnished brass plaque on the street, with his titles written out. Probably, in this old French neighborhood, he wanted to avoid revealing the "ski" that ended his name and to stop himself from taking on more patients. He didn't chase money and limited his time in the office to three or four hours each afternoon. His patients were mostly older women who had been faithful clients for years, with an attachment to him that was almost romantic. They revered him. At least he didn't throw them out after five minutes. He talked to them for a long time, like old friends. This man who said nothing to his immediate family spoke to his patients with real warmth. He took their troubles seriously, their migraines, their insomnia, their chronic aches and pains. He called them his "little crazies," people with illnesses that were benign and most likely caused by neuroses. But no sooner did they develop a worrying symptom, beyond their usual complaints, no sooner did they fall gravely ill, which was bound to happen eventually, than he pronounced his incompetence, called for expertise outside his own, and rushed to hand them off to a colleague.

6

On the mantel in the office, his shiny awards glimmered like decorations on the chest of a Russian general. Round and rectangular, smooth or striped, they were imposing in their density, their thickness. They displayed Minerva's face in her helmet, a pensive Pasteur, a healing Hygiene. But mostly Marianne, a France devoted to knowledge and admiration. These pieces of metal rewarded the path of gifted scholarship, showered with successes, a university education without a single mistake, an exemplary career. First prize in silver, diploma coated in bronze. A worthy youth, paid in cash. The coin of the Republic, sometimes held in security at the municipal bank when we were broke. Like the medal for his internship, the most precious of all of them. The only object I inherited from him. A hundred grams of pure gold awarded in 1928 and pawned more than once before and during the war. Every medal has its downside. All these coin-shaped prizes lined up next to the telephone on the gray marble slab, facing the mirror, forming a sort of altar to public education, to Jules Ferry and his good works.

7

That's all I know about his childhood. This wholesome story, told many times, of successful assimilation and a rapid rise in society thanks to republican schooling. The couple from Russia, languishing in poverty in Batignolles. Changing apartments with the rhythm of the pay cycle. A tiny loft, an unsanitary ground floor, and finally three rooms looking out on the courtyard, and then facing the street. The father, a laborer at a carriage company, coming back late at night or early in the morning, exhausted, as worn out from work as from the long periods of unemployment. The mother, still in shock at her brutal loss of status, disappointed, distraught, fleeing into the past or the future from a present that she finds sad and vulgar. The only child who becomes her avatar in a world with a language and rules she doesn't understand. A good boy. She listens with pride to him reciting "our ancestors, the Gauls," in a Faubourg accent; she'll place her unfulfilled ambition in him, her unquenched thirst for a second try. A good little French boy in breeches, noticed by his teachers, always the first and already alone, ready to leave his game of jacks or marbles so he can rush home to do his assignments. A string of scholarships from the city of Paris. And, at the end of the year, the honor roll, prizes, handsome books, medals given in front of admiring parents who, in all the commotion, don't understand anything but his name, their own, solemnly spoken in the school courtyard.

But was it their own? When I ask the people around me this simple question, I get embarrassed and contradictory answers. I'm unable to outline their identity completely. They are almost anonymous, with lives that consist of a handful of anecdotes. And for Niania, an exotic nickname. For one purpose. She claimed to be one of the Macagons. At least to her ears it was a Russian-sounding name that filled her with pride, as if it contained an honorific. I'm spelling it phonetically, because it doesn't appear on any official document. I should put it in quotations, because its authenticity has always seemed doubtful. Her French friends, her acquaintances, and later, her coworkers, all called her Hélène. The Frenchified version of Helena. And her husband? The forefather? The Stentor of Odessa? His early death makes his existence even more ghostly, because it happened before the family moved into the Rue-de-Grenelle, before we began to blend in with its walls. In this story, he hangs like a shadow in the background. Before I began my research, I didn't even know his first name. My father had forgotten it. Christian, after a short pause, said "David." David Boltanski.

8

They had only one point of entry: their son. They were born with him into the administrative and social world. Before, in the eyes of French law, they were nothing, or not much. Two foreigners with their papers more or less in order. In Paris, the city records from 1860 to 1902 are digitized. You can look them up online. A window in the top left of the screen lets you zoom in on the part of the text you need. The family name appears in the margin, written in cursive, with the upward and downward strokes of the pen, the twisted capital letters, and the sinuous letter *s* that everyone learns in grade school.

> In the year eighteen ninety-six, the fifth of March, at three-thirty in the afternoon, birth certificate for the male child Étienne Boltanski, born the third of this month at two in the morning, 105 avenue de Saint-Ouen, son of David Boltanski, aged 41, upholsterer, and Enta Fainstein, aged 25, no profession, married, living at 101 rue de Tocqueville. Prepared by Léon Henri Thiébaut, Deputy Mayor, officer of the civil government of the 17th arrondissement of Paris, Chevalier of the Legion of Honor, upon the presentation of the child and the declaration of the Father, in the presence of Jacques Lebedinsky, aged 24, medical student residing at 5 rue Lalande, and of Martin Redon, aged 33, day laborer, residing at 101 rue de Tocqueville, witnesses who have signed with us and the declaring party upon reading.

Despite the bureaucratic dryness, I have the impression of looking at a photo. Three intimidated men facing a functionary, imposing with his red-banded tailcoat and managerial jargon. The one with the baby in his arms is David. I didn't imagine him so old. Forty-one. A late age to leave everything behind—

his country, his family, his customs—and embark on a new
life. By his side, two witnesses chosen out of desperation. Mar-
tin Redon, a neighbor, because he lived at the same address,
101 rue de Tocqueville. But who was Jacques Lebedinsky? No
doubt a compatriot. A friend, cousin, or just someone he knew.
Because of his studies, he had mastered French and could help
deal with the authorities. And one person missing: the mother,
still in bed, whose maiden name was not Hélène Macagon but
Enta Fainstein. At least not according to this paper.

Where is the truth in it all? Identity documents can be falsified, especially in czarist Russia, to avoid military service or
to cross borders, to escape the pale of settlement and live in
Moscow or Saint Petersburg. I only have one other source to
go on: the dusty folds of pages, sometimes still uncut, carefully shelved in the office bookcase and signed Annie Lauran.
Of course, these are novels. It's obviously wrong to take them
for anything other than works of literature, to read them like
minutes or legal depositions, to judge author by narrator, to
confuse her baroque characters and their doings in real life,
to force her work into a single, literal interpretation, to pretend that they spring, fully cooked, from reality and not from
her imagination. *Et cetera.* But how can you not connect Étienne Boltanski and "Louis Gatowsky," the hero of *Saturday's
Cake*, a "a promising physician" brooded over by his mother,
that woman "always dressed in black" who arrived in Paris "one
winter evening" with "a samovar under her arm"? Or "Michel
Barsky," described in *The Woman I Once Was* as a "serious, sen-
sible, innocent" young man "with a tanned face and wavy black
hair" who also lived with his mother? Or even the child in *Resucideception*, "born so fast, the child with slanted eyes, not like
the ones here," "the son of Hélène, of ignorant Enta with long
brown hair who came from Odessa, looking for her freedom?"

My grandmother's books, inspired by her in-laws, reveal that most of the information they gave officials was crawling with errors, willful or not. The father isn't named David but Ilya or Ilioucha. Élie in Russian. Like his grandson, whom he never met. The mother is named Enta, or Entele, Fainstein, or at least that's the name on her passport, and not Hélène Macagon, as she claims. She also lies about her age. She's not twenty-five. It's clear already that she was much younger, maybe even a minor. She left everything—her town, her country, her family, her comfort, for a man who was old enough to be her father. The couple lived at 105 avenue de Saint-Ouen, writes Annie Lauran, between the city gate and the "little belt" railway that surrounded Paris, in a "stinking ground-floor apartment," occupied today by a rotisserie butcher shop and a hair salon. Or was she talking about the next floor up, lit by minuscule windows? In one of these recessed arrow slits, you can just glimpse a plaster bust of Marianne, her face peering into the glass, as if the Republic had decided after all to turn away from this sad and cacophonous back street, its lines of chestnut trees leading to the flea market. So who lived in 100 Rue de Tocqueville, a Haussmann-style apartment building in a classier neighborhood, now flanked by a Chinese restaurant, a few steps from the porte d'Asnières?

My grandfather always said that the family name he gave us contained an error. According to him, it was misspelled by the French immigration services, and by the rules of transliterating Cyrillic into the Latin alphabet, it should have ended with a *y*, not an *i*. Boltanski presumably came from the name of a place: Balta, a city located 113 miles northwest of Odessa, with a population that was mostly Jewish until World War II, a city that had been Ottoman, Polish, Russian, Soviet, Romanian, and finally Ukrainian. Many other spellings would have been possible in Eastern Europe, where names changed constantly at the mercy of conquests and redrawn borders: Boltanskij, Baltanski, Baltansky, Baltyanski, Baltyansky, Baltyyanski, Baltyyanskij, Boltyanski, Boltyansky, Boltyanskik . . . grand-papa's insistence on this rather harmless mistake, in light of his family, thickly couched in mystery, makes me think there's something more in that last letter than a muffled sound. Something that reveals an identity.

9

At school, Étienne was proud to be Russian. Russian like Nicholas II, crossing Paris in a carriage beside President Félix Faure, whom the press sarcastically called Felixkoff. Russian like the czarist fleet showing off in Toulon's harbor or the Saint Petersburg balls in honor of Republican dignitaries. Russian like the bear crowned with caricatures, Kaiser Wilhelm's nightmare. Russian like the little girl in white who decorated the Exquis Guillout cookie boxes or the "bonbonof ruskof" sweets sold on the boulevards. Like the stock everyone wants to sell, these securities in faded colors, in rubles, would soon be no more than bits of paper. To his awestruck classmates, he belonged to the powerful empire that allowed France to come out of isolation, to the empire that would terrorize Germany as everyone hoped and make another war impossible. His head was filled with clichés, with picture postcards and stamps celebrating the Franco-Russian alliance, displaying serene bearded men with fringed epaulettes and two-headed eagles on a gold background. He lived in an imaginary world peopled with cossacks at full gallop, messengers for the czar, and Michel Strogoff holding off the tartar hordes.

Until one hot, sunny afternoon in spring. His second birth.

He was nine years old. Unlike most days, his mother met him after school. She called him her little king and stroked his hair as they went down the avenue de Villiers. How do I know these details? The scene is carefully reported in *Saturday's Cake* and *Resucideception*. I've also heard it told many times as a joke. Étienne was laughing, letting go of her hand to run around plucking green leaves that poked through the grates. When he handed his mother this tousled bouquet, she took him in her arms and squeezed him hard against her embroidered white blouse. Belle époque Paris surrounded them. Horses passed, whips cracked. Hats strolled down the street. She forced a smile, her voice strange. The first time, he didn't understand the question. "You don't hate Jews, do you?" she repeated. She was hurting him a little, practically suffocating him. To get out of her grip, and also because he was a good boy, kind to everyone, he replied "No" in his good-student voice, anxious to give the right answer. He saw his mother's face immediately relax. She kissed him on the forehead, saying, "Ah! I'm so glad. Because your Papa and I, we're Jewish. You're a Jew, my darling boy."

Other images poured into his mind. Cartoons glimpsed in the same newspapers that celebrated big brother Russia. Bogeymen with thick lips and sagging necks along with countless stories that were funny, or supposed to be, in almanacs or calendars. Posters, intended to frighten, plastering the streets the night before an election, warning of an invisible enemy. He remembered insults shouted at cheaters, epithets spat during recess by his classmates with such conviction, as if they were based on evidence. Maybe even from his own mouth. He felt sick. She was shocked at his paleness and decided to offer him a little treat for his snack. Maybe she wanted to mark the event. He wasn't hungry. She had to drag him to the pastry shop on the place Pereire and scold him so he didn't drop his cherry tart on the tiled floor of the shop.

10

He had a twin, a double, but turned inside out. Same origins, same age down to the month, same studies, but two personalities, fates that differed like fire and water. Théodore Fraenkel was his shadow, his opposite, his good little devil. The one he could have been. In Odessa, their fathers had known each other. They were basically neighbors. Théodore's father was the first to immigrate to Paris. David or Eliahou—whatever his first name was—had he followed this example? Their two boys found themselves on the same benches at Chaptal, a modern school, meaning they didn't teach Latin and Greek, on the boulevard des Batignolles. They both wanted to become writers. Étienne read Alphonse Daudet, Jules Renard, Pierre Loti. Scholarly writers, very French, destined for the Académie française, reputable enough to be given out at the end of the year. Books that were school prizes. No doubt the ones he had received. His companion displayed tastes that were riskier: Mallarmé, Huysmans, Baudelaire. Alfred Jarry, above all. He pretended to be Ubu. He spouted bizarre words, mangled other sounds, created homonyms, composed pastiches and acrostics, busied himself with anagrams. He could also be a prankster, telling incredible tall tales that got him in heaps of trouble. Fédia, as Étienne called him, was kind, funny, cruel. He was his best friend and also his worst bully, endlessly mocking his seriousness and his helpless side. Théodore quickly found another supporter: a young oracle with a high forehead and slow gestures. In his autobiography, André Breton says he noticed Fraenkel when he was a student because of the way he recited verses. Breton was apparently seduced by his disenchanted grimaces, his shrugs, his fierce spirit and cold irony. The two high schoolers shared a passion for poetry, the bizarre, dark humor, provocation, anarchy, the illegal. They worshipped Jules Bonnot and his band of thieves in cars, whose slightest misdeeds were reported in *Le Petit Journal*. After classes, they strolled around the Gustave Moreau museum and fantasized about the glimmering naiads of long ago. They stuck together until they were forced to part ways.

While he was never a Dadaist or surrealist, Étienne was a part of what could be considered the core of the original Bretonesque avant-garde: The Sophists' Club. A group of brats that already had the characteristics of groups to come—closed meetings, chosen disciples, and a mastermind. André Breton was of course the leader; Théodore Fraenkel was his right-hand man. I don't know what role my grandfather played. I have a lot of trouble imagining him as a devotee, cultivating eloquence, and even more difficulty associating him with hilarious evenings soaked in absinthe. I don't believe he contributed to their poetry magazine run by René Hilsum, the future editor of *Sans Pareil*. In 1913, all three of them enrolled in premed courses and began medical school the next year. By default, since none of them really had a calling, and with perfect togetherness, as if they were inseparable. I don't know whose idea it was. Of the three, quiet Étienne stands out. Unless he was once a completely different person? A burning spirit, inventive, sure of himself, and—why not—audacious?

11

When and how had he been broken? The first time was the same for millions of men: feet in the mud, facing a soft mound of earth piled with different kinds of waste, with wooden barriers and gnarled bushes of barbed wire; in a narrow ditch, subjected to violent trembling, giving off a smell of piss, shit, sweat, and butchered meat. You could write a whole book about his two years in the trenches if he had passed on his memories, kept a journal, saved his letters, even if they were redacted by the censor. But he left nothing. During his lifetime he was equally reserved. As soon as we questioned him about his war, he invariably sent us to read Henri Barbusse's *Under Fire*. As if Barbusse, who was sent home for health reasons in 1916, just as my grandfather was being mobilized, had already said everything: the bodies covered in dirt, dazed, bent over, their noses between their knees, boots sticking in the clay, intense cold, waiting, the wail of missiles, the whistling of shrapnel, the thundering of heavy artillery, the slow sigh of the no. 75 shells, all this auditory skill that allowed them to guess whether they would live or die, the panicked fear when they stepped over the fortifications, the lunar desert between the two enemy lines, huge, full of water, crossed with ruts and pierced with beams, plywood boards and tangles of iron, holes piled with corpses that they stumbled over or found hanging, crucified on the barbed wire, turned into scarecrows with arms stretched out, the constant screaming of the wounded in the night, the friend you almost recognize in the unmoving monster planted in the soil, his eyes cooked, a wreck.

He could've had an exemption because of his studies. "If you don't go off to fight and come back decorated, then you're no son of mine," his mother warned him. And he made it happen, as they say. Did he allow himself to be swayed by patriotic folly? Or, after two years of carnage, did he already sense that this insane firestorm was destroying Europe? He was careful to obey his mother's order without having to give his life. Instead of volunteering, he ignored the call, knowing that he would be drafted. One morning, the police came to get him. The army dumped him in the medical corps and attached him to the 54th Infantry, commanding a unit of stretcher-bearers. He was sent to the front on November 21, 1916.

He was in charge of a first aid station, a hole covered with boards and two feet of rocky earth, with the red cross flag on top. A privileged place to observe modern mass killing, industrial, violent, and anonymous. In that chain of extermination, he was only a powerless link. Without penicillin, which wasn't discovered until 1928, he could only apply cursory bandages or strips of plaster. Then he quickly filled out a form and pinned it to the dying man's clothes. Name, regiment, nature of wound, whether or not a tetanus shot had been administered. He followed the methods that were taught at Val-de-Grâce Hospital in those days, based on the experience of previous battles. Since the bullets had been disinfected by fire, war wounds were said to be antiseptic. To avoid contamination, they weren't supposed to touch them. Medical units had to content themselves with staunching hemorrhages, stopping the flow of blood, splinting fractures, and moving the patient as far from the front lines as possible. Before understanding this error, the military academy did not advise surgical intervention. The poilu, they assured, would heal himself. They realized belatedly that three quarters of injuries were caused by exploding shells, which mixed with mud, stagnant water, and the dirty cloth of uniform jackets, causing immediate infections. After traveling for several days in jostling ambulances, and then on crowded trains, most of the severely wounded arrived at the hospitals with tetanus or suppurating gangrene.

The *Record of Marches and Operations* kept by his unit and

now available on the Internet does not describe the horrors flowing into the infirmary with their faces covered in dirt, their intestines hanging out, their bloody stumps and half buttocks, their larynxes torn as if someone had slit their throats, still able to make sounds despite their open skulls revealing curves of scarlet brain. It also doesn't mention the conditions inside the shelter: the wounded grabbing your shirt and demanding to be taken care of first, the spouts of vomit, ether, and hot gunk, the acetylene lamp going out every time a "Big Bertha" falls nearby, the ground cut through with water and blood, the muddy fingers digging in dimness for the wound and dousing it with iodine tincture, the dead piled up outside, swollen and covered with flies, the dull hammering every half second, which throws you to the floor and threatens to turn the ward into a tomb. Nothing about the whistle blasts, the shouts of "forward march!" from the officers, the despairing race after the first wave of the assault, the clacking of machine guns, the cries, the explosions, the bodies that are too heavy to lift, the stretcher dragged through the muck, the stretcher-bearers dying one after another, with nothing to send home, just red slush, like my grandfather's best friend, the son of a Jewish shopkeeper from Roubaix whom everyone called "Fileuzeuf," not because of his capacity to make up theories but because of his sangfroid in all situations. Not a word, either, about the worst winter of the war. Oh wait! A few understatements as days go by. November 26, 1916: "Sanitary conditions are poor (many relieved of duty for frostbitten feet)." December 10, 1916: "Change of guard in the night, without incident, but very painful because of rain and mud." January 15, 1917: "18-mile march, cold weather." Even war is described with the tone of a weather report, as though they were experiencing a series of storms. From March 10 to

19 of the same year: "Enemy artillery quiet at first, becoming more and more active. . . . The thaw makes the trenches and passageways almost impassable."

On the other hand, this logbook allows me to follow Étienne's footsteps with the precision of a GPS, to go with him on each of his transfers, to know the destinations, his swings back and forth, his encampments, his movements up the line with the rhythm of offensives, his marches and retreats, most often undertaken at night, crushing, impossible for this man who wasn't a walker. Giant cemeteries. The Somme, first of all, at the end of 1916. A million victims. Bois-l'Abbé farm, Malassies ridge, Bouchavesnes ravine, Riez wood, Fargny mill. Farm, ravine, wood, mill, which are already nothing more than points on the military staff maps, nothing but the chaos of ruins and decapitated trunks. Then the Chemin des Dames, from January to mid-May 1917. Five hundred thousand dead, on both sides. Soupir, Moussy, Braisne, Hauzy wood, Saint-Mard, Montagne farm, Ostel, Château Ruiné, the Gargousse, Chevregny ridge, the caves of Coblentz. Behind these names, a tormented plateau, slopes of jagged grottos, and, at the top, the impregnable Hindenburg line. And as many mass graves as charges. Attacks whose obvious absurdity strikes the men in charge like so many shells. Ranges too short, objectives too far away, makeshift tactics spoiled before they were even put into action. Did he witness the first acts of mutiny? Did he also imagine deserting, fleeing this pointless killing?

Such a traumatic experience couldn't be communicated. Walter Benjamin traces the disappearance of the storyteller to the First World War. Because, he explains, it's death that transforms life into a tale. Death alone curates a life of assorted images and gives them an order resembling fate. No epics, no heroic couplets without an exemplary death. But as soon as it becomes anonymous, reduced to a mechanical operation, death can no longer perform its sanctioning role nor create the material from which stories are made. The soldiers of 1914, glorified as unknowns because they had been reduced to abundant and interchangeable human parts, came back silent from the battlefield. He was like the rest. His service records, filed at the Paris City Hall archive, indicate a Croix de Guerre dated August 1, 1917. That particular decoration was never displayed on the office mantel.

12

It rested inside a huge Louis-Phillipe writing desk built of walnut and placed almost in the center of the room. Well hidden— behind the flap, in the back of a compartment. Maybe forgotten to this day, in a nook of that desk that was full of surprises, where young ladies from previous centuries hid their gallant correspondence. All you had to do was push a button or pull a lever—I don't remember which anymore—to open a secret compartment concealed behind a decorative panel. My grandfather arranged minute objects in these little drawers, things without monetary or aesthetic value that carried a heavy sentimental weight. By their juxtaposition, they took on meaning and allowed a glimpse into his internal universe, or else, his interior chaos. With the great discoveries of the Renaissance, both learned men and princes used curio cabinets to create representations of the world. As the precursors of modern museums, they housed incredible bric-a-brac—from the turban of the grand eunuch of Constantinople to the head of a Cyclops, Egyptian mummies, Mexican codices, or bezoars, those stones found in the gizzards of animals that supposedly have all kinds of magical qualities. And also medals, ancient coins, parchment papers, money resting in compartments that opened with artfully concealed inner mechanisms. My grandfather's interior display held only one form of oddity: war.

Besides the Croix de Guerre, the writing desk was a jumble that contained his yellow star (which also provoked the maid to say, in ignorance or cruelty, "I saw a gentleman in the street with a cockade like monsieur's, but it looks much better on you"), papers forged by one of his friends, a surgeon who under the circumstances became expert at it, a newspaper folded in quarters he showed me one afternoon, exhuming it from the drawer after his last patient had gone. He must have thought I was old enough to grasp what it meant, that word in all caps, printed in fat black type, that repeated in every line, before or after slurs: "lice-ridden," "profiteer," "parasite," "negroid," "undesirable," "invader," or "crook." Unlike today's weeklies, *Au Pilori*'s job wasn't to inform. As the name suggests, it denounced. For those who were vindictive, or worse, violent, it targeted a specific population. The issue was dated August 16, 1940. Under the headline "Let's Purify France!," a cartoon showed a man with a hooked nose, a cigar in his mouth, and a pocket watch hanging over his fat stomach admiring, with a well-fed air, a battlefield covered in French corpses. Lists of individuals followed, organized by profession and always introduced with the same word in all caps. Two months after the fall of France, *Au Pilori* began its smear campaign with the most sensitive professions, those most likely to influence bodies and minds. On page two, they published a list of Jewish doctors and professors who were prominent members of the Paris public hospital system. For Saint-Antoine Hospital, eight names were cited. His was one of them.

13

Did someone give it to him or did he rush out to buy it at the kiosk on the boulevard Raspail? I imagine him inspecting the paper, running his finger down the column with the same feverishness he felt when he searched through test results in the halls of the medical school on the boulevard Saint-Germain. After the shock passed, he probably tried to reassure himself. This list is not unfamiliar to him. How many times has he found his last name erased from the rounds schedule, replaced by the words *dirty jew* scribbled in chalk? Good marks given year after year on his evaluations—"excellent student, worthy of promotion to intern," "very good resident in all aspects," "very thoughtful intern, conscientious"—make no difference. From the very beginning of medical school, he prepared for an exam he couldn't pass. When he came in second on the written exams for medical certification, his supervisor convinced him not to take the oral: "It's no good," he told him, "You won't be chosen. They already selected a Jew last year." The Deposits and Consignments Fund rejected his application for a position as their in-house doctor. They didn't even consider his candidacy. "We're in a very difficult spot," the director wrote to him, "We would have been happy to employ you, but we hear that you're an Israelite."

Habit led him to underestimate the threat. He wanted to believe it was just another outbreak of a chronic illness he knew all too well. His surroundings—hospitals, accredited, supposedly immaculate—nurtured a virulent anti-Semitism. In between the wars, he tried to ignore this hatred that kept on growing. The jokes from medical students about his "greaser's hair" and the heated demonstrations outside the building, calls to deport "mixed breeds," the pressure, at union meetings, to drive him and those like him out of public health, the offhand comments from his distinguished colleagues about people who "cheat their clients" and take the place of "real Frenchmen," or the article by "Dr. Bosc," published in the *Paris Journal of Medical Residents*, blasting the "hordes of Huns," the "unlikely transplants from the Levant," ready to "attack French medicine," including—already—lists of Jewish students who should be kicked out.

14

His veteran status allows him to escape the first Vichy edicts that forbid Jews from being civil servants and therefore from working in hospitals. After that, they limit Jewish doctors to 2 percent of the medical profession. For a time, he keeps practicing at Saint-Antoine. He's already nothing more than a man on borrowed time, stripped of his managerial status and gilded stripes, then reduced to sewing his star onto his white coat. "It's perfectly normal for you to wear a distinctive marking," one of his interns explains to him in an erudite tone. "In the Middle Ages, didn't your people already wear the rota?" He keeps seeing patients at his house, in fewer and fewer numbers. He can no longer make appointments. His telephone has been confiscated as well as his car and his wireless radio. He goes out as little as possible. After August, 1941, they round up French nationals as well as foreigners. He knows he could be arrested and sent to Drancy, that place north of Paris everyone's been talking about, a horseshoe-shaped structure surrounded by watchtowers. "What are you doing, doctor?" a sick patient asks, looking him in the eye. He was sitting, in the middle of writing a prescription, when all of a sudden, he disappeared from sight. The woman bends over and finds him crouching on the ground. Hearing the doorbell, he'd taken fright and plunged under his antique desk.

In the course of a meeting on December 3, 1942, with a M. Brodin presiding, the board of oversight for Paris public hospitals decides to put on unpaid leave three members of the staff who, "for diverse reasons have not been on duty for quite some time." The personnel affected by these measures are "M. Boltanski, doctor, Chief of Staff at Saint-Antoine hospital, René Bloch, surgeon, Chief of Staff at Saint-Vincent-de-Paul hospice, M. Maduro, ear, nose, and throat specialist."

15

The prefect of police's signature had been faked in purple ink. And the seal of the French State, no doubt carved in linoleum. The identification card was real, because that part was easy. All the libraries sold them. The cardholder bought it blank and took it to the police station. It had a four-numeral date of issue on the top left and a thirteen-franc stamp from a similarly fabricated mold. The physical features were as close as possible to the truth. Height, five feet, three inches. Hair, brown. Brown eyes. Square nose. Olive skin tone. Face shape, oval. The name had been chosen to avoid suspicion as much as possible. Giraud sounds very French. It's a common name, without being overused. But the first name might surprise you. Jeanine. And in the black-and-white photo on the card, grand-papa is wearing a wavy wig that falls to his shoulders, a pearl necklace, and what looks like a silk dress. In this getup, he bears a vague resemblance to a manly Miss Marple. "It might still come in handy!" he would say with a cunning smile whenever someone pulled these papers out of the drawer. Had he ever used them? I don't see how he could have fooled anyone with such an outrageous disguise.

Parlor

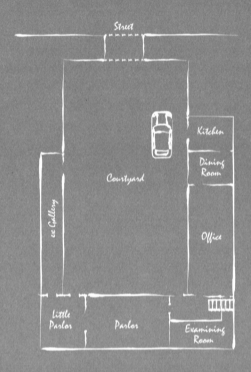

1

There are two of them. The smaller one leans his ear to the door, peering up through the glass canopy. The other one paces the courtyard. Just as they are about to get a locksmith, she opens the door for them. "Well-dressed Frenchmen, with very sweet faces," she wrote years later. The first takes care to wipe his feet on the worn straw mat and to take off his hat before entering. The other keeps his large gray fedora on his head. She explains to them that her husband no longer lives there. She doesn't know where he has gone. Besides, they're divorced. She orders her son, Jean-Élie, to go get the papers that prove it. The police officers ask to search the house. They follow her with heavy steps that echo down the long parquet corridor. The parlor and the little parlor are linked to the outside by a gallery that runs along the right wing of the building, which will soon be given over to the neighbors. She walks slowly, leaning on furniture and on the window sills. The two men in black coats who follow her begin to look impatient. Their orders are strict. The July 13, 1942, ordinance tells them to "proceed as quickly as possible, without useless conversation and without commentary." Did they report to the Bureau of Investigations, or were they sent by the police station on the rue Perronet? They conclude that this room, which had been a waiting room weeks earlier, is now a pantry. They almost stumble over the jars of food piled between two armchairs covered with dust. Used to tracking the black market, they probably cast a suspicious look at a big metal basin, pressing against the glass, where globules of white eggs soak in salty water. After a moment that seems like an eternity, they leave empty handed.

2

Christmases pass without the father around a tree topped, scornfully, with his yellow star. Already Luc has trouble remembering this man who used to take him to the Tuileries and watch him through the bars of a park he wasn't allowed to enter. His mother promises that father will return, bearing loads of gifts, but nobody comes down the chimney. Only the sudden screaming of sirens, faraway explosions like thunderclaps, and, at the appointed hour, the orderly hammering of boots on asphalt break the silence in the house. War continues as background noise, filtered through the panels of the gate. Born into it, the child listens for its slightest sound. He almost never goes out. Confined to this long series of somber, empty rooms, he keeps his nose pressed to the glass, trying to guess what could be happening on the other side of the courtyard. For hours, he gazes at the closed, stony space. He lets himself be rocked by the whisper of the street and butchers the song "Lili Marlène," which the soldiers hum as they march. Sometimes he catches a glimpse of them from the doorway, their stiff legs, their dogs on leashes, and applauds like he's at a show. His brother looks on with disapproval.

3

It was a devastated landscape: paper walls sliced with scissors, sketched doorframes, halves of windows. As if the little houses had been decapitated by an enormous scythe. Two encircling ramparts, pierced with arrow slits, were equipped in places with a parapet walk on the top. Like dirty snow, whitish wood pulp coated lanes dotted with rubble. For watchtowers, little bits of roof balanced on blackened matchsticks. Train tracks climbed to a Vauban-like citadel perched on a hill. A bluish stream ran through the middle, and, like the Seine does in Paris, the water encircled a tiny island at the sharpest part of the curve. The defenders were usually Nazis squeezed from polystyrene, mousy gray, no bigger than a finger. The attackers were the same size, but made from green plastic, and belonging to various allied armies. These figures reduced to seventy-second scale were sold in boxes of forty by the brand Airfix. I carefully kept the packaging printed with war scenes. One of them showed marines disembarking on a Pacific island, another American parachutists landing in a wasted field, some kneeling and others still in the air. My favorite displayed British commandos in striped wool caps, about to board their boats and attack a chalky cliff.

The bombed-out town took up almost a quarter of the surface area in the parlor. It was built on paintings my uncle finished as a teenager which had been stored in the cellar. Like Van Gogh painted over his canvases to save money, Christian used his juvenilia as a base for our battles. Before they disappeared under a mass of glue, cardboard, and other debris, they were six big plywood boards evoking scenes of cities, generally in flames. Like ancient citadels, razed and rebuilt many times over, our rubble also rested on other ruins. Christian destroyed his old paintings, masking them, chewing them up, not in the name of experimentation, like Duchamp's explorations of the fourth dimension, the passing of time, but more out of a desire to reject his early figurative period and to feed his taste for the fragile, the ephemeral, the futility of human activity, which coexisted with attempts to remake his childhood memories in modeling clay.

We followed precise rules for maneuvers and engagements.

Each turn, the infantry advanced three feet and the motorized divisions six. We fired with ten centime or five franc coins, depending on which weapons were used. The skirmishes set hundreds of men against each other and dozens of tanks and cannons, fighter planes, bombers. The models smelled of turpentine and strong glue. They were half broken from the rain of blows. We spent whole afternoons here, Wednesdays, weekends, and holidays. Some of our battles lasted for days. They stretched across the whole room and sometimes all the way to the little parlor. The Persian rugs with faded colors became seas or rivers forded by battleships and unloading naval vessels. Erector sets and a colorful wooden sculpture by André Cadere—one of his first, a square bar, since a round one wouldn't have worked—were our movable bridges. Pieces of linen fabric thrown over books were impassable mountains; antique dressers, the prie-dieu, the Directoire sofa, the marble hearth of the fireplace, the table legs all created natural obstacles and hiding places where forces in great numbers could patiently await the enemy.

In this space of antiquated, almost absurd solemnity, with its ancient furniture and glasswork, we created an alternate universe. A violent, yes, but perfectly ordered microcosm where we were the commanders in chief. These battlefields satisfied our need for escape and our claustrophilia, our impulses toward both travel and hiding. Usually, I emerged victorious. I think Christian, out of kindness, set it up so I would win. Perhaps he also wanted to see his own forces defeated? I always picked the Allies, and he was left with the Axis powers. He claims he learned a lot about his work by playing with toy soldiers. About the irony of miniature, about the ability of tiny objects to accumulate into monuments, about falseness that allows access to a deeper truth, about the ties between childhood and death.

He liked to destroy his creations, like those towns built of cardboard and sugar cubes, which we burned when we were finished with them. Once they were released into the fire, the little white bricks melted and bubbled, giving off a smell of burned caramel. Those innocent houses looked ridiculous when they were standing—their triangle tops and their windows drawn with one black line. But they became dramatic as they were consumed, which gave us a kind of Neronian pleasure. Until the end of adolescence, Christian was my main if not my only playmate along with my aunt, Anne, who was almost my age. In the middle of my third year of lycée, I decided to give my whole collection of models to a boy named Roland, the nephew of one of my father's friends, and a few months later, I became a little soldier, enlisting in a Communist youth group.

The building, which had been designed for one noble family, was poorly suited for apartments that served several purposes. I had to abandon my troops every time the doorbell rang in the little parlor. The metallic brriiing and the dry click of the lock were the signals to flee. For a while, the glass door was operated from a distance by a man in a white uniform, the twin of Nestor from Moulinsart Castle, who never left his half-moon-shaped table at the back of the foyer and never relaxed his stiff bearing. At the beginning of the seventies, the clients became fewer and fewer, and M. Roger (that was his name) disappeared. The patients terrified me, as if they carried the plague or cholera. As soon as they entered the house, I'd retreat to the upper floors. I never saw them. All I can remember is the glass of the window, their silhouettes against it, and their voices, tight and resigned, coming through the panels of the office. During consulting hours, the lower rooms were off limits in order to preserve the quiet of a medical practice. The forbidden areas included the kitchen and the dining room, which were inaccessible anyway, except through the garden. We had to make as little noise as possible and stay hidden until the last of the invaders had gone.

5

Because of this rule, the parlor created a hybrid space at the frontier of intimate and social, inside and outside, work and play, suffering and ease. It was a professional place, a reception room, a setting of symbolic prestige, frozen in its Faubourg Saint-Germain decor. The peeling paint and bubbling plaster only intensified the sense that it was fake. Crawling on all fours, my eyes always fixed on my miniature world, I forgot what was over my head. I only have a fuzzy image of murals, sconces, sculpted pillars with gilded edging, and wallpaper painted with streamers. More than anything I remember the blue carpet thrown over the sagging floor, giving the impression of a flat surface. It was a theater where we acted out a vaudeville sketch. A farce with the main goal of bringing a succession of people onto the scene in a more and more frenetic whirlwind—husband, lover, cheating wife—who would be scandalized to run into each other. The room didn't fill with shouts or slamming doors. But it welcomed different, nearly contradictory publics, whose inevitable encounters produced an odd, almost burlesque effect. During those years, only our soldiers maintained a constant presence. I've wondered ever since if, in the middle of all that splendor, our ruined cities upset those visitors who came to learn whether they were sick or well.

6

The invitations didn't come from the doctor but from his spouse. He ran from human contact; she cultivated it. She claimed it was all for him, to interest him, for his pleasure, though she was the only one who shone among her friends, her faithful she passed off as *his*. She was the queen, or else the regent of evenings that she organized in his name, despite his resistance. She hosted people like him, emerging, as he was, dazed from a dark night, who turned toward him out of politeness and spoke only to her. He listened to them, wearing his perpetual smile that contained a hint of irony. Even if he preferred to be alone, he held them in high esteem. They would have been his friends if he'd had any. There were several among them who were his interns, some doctors, psychologists. Many were involved, like him, with the National Institute for the Study of Work and Professional Practice, the Inetop, a research lab which was a longtime Communist bastion. But it wasn't their careers, often newfound, tied, like everything else, to circumstance, which brought them together. All of them had changed their lives, their names, their professions, sometimes their families. They aspired only to security. They weren't sure of anything. This atmosphere, grand as it was, had a feeling of passing through that suited these people in transit, people who were ready to cut and run with no destination in mind, as if their suitcases were always packed. In that waiting room, they were finally at home.

Eugène Bencz had a small wholesale business. He bought books on clearance from publishers and sold them to libraries and community organizations. His store was on the corner of the rue Guynemer and the rue de Fleurus, facing the entrance to the Luxembourg gardens. Apart from the Fiat, my grandmother had no space to herself, and she sometimes went to work at his shop in the mornings. He was ashamed to be a business man and thought of himself as an intellectual. Before the war, he'd finished a PhD in philosophy at the University of Toulouse and published an anthology of nineteenth-century Hungarian poetry with Éditions de la Renaissance. From time to time, he invited my family to eat with him at Czardas, a restaurant on the rue Lafayette.

Adolphe Nuchi owned a factory that made plastic handbags he sold at markets. He was one of the first to import sewing machines for fake leather. A funny sort of boss, who encouraged his employees to vote Communist every election. He was also a sculptor and the director of *Osmose*, a poetry magazine, with Bernard Citroën, another prominent figure in Saint-Germain-des-Prés, the man in the green cape who went on vacation with my grandparents. Adolphe was passionate about literature, wrote prose pieces, and introduced mère-grand to books by Henry Miller and Georges Bataille. She met him through his wife, Alice, or maybe Alice's mother, the woman she bought her shoes from. An old woman who barely spoke French. She had a stall at the Swiss Village, the area between the avenues de la Motte-Picquet and de Suffren created for the World Exhibition, which became a secondhand market after the grand Ferris wheel was demolished in 1937.

Zina Morhange hadn't practiced medicine since Auschwitz. She owned a clothing store in Marseille that she'd inherited after her second husband, Joe Saltiel, committed suicide. As soon as she could, she left that hated business behind and returned to Paris. Her brother-in-law, the poet Pierre Morhange, was also a member of the circle. These visits were among his rare outings. After the Holocaust and after Stalin's anti-Semitic response to the Plot of the White Shirts, he only rarely left his apartment on the rue Saint-Augustin. He was a surrealist before joining the Communists, so he'd broken with two camps in a row. Because of his exclusion, he lived like a recluse. He came with Motia, his wife, a postimpressionist painter from Odessa, and with Joseph Constantinovsky, her brother, who sculpted animals under the pseudonym Joseph Constant and wrote novels inspired by Isaac Babel under the name of Michel Matveev. A triple identity, crafted to get people off his trail.

She gathered them together for "little nothing dinners," as the Duchesse de Guermantes would say, except that in her case, there really was next to nothing. She served rolls with liver pâté, but never enough for each guest, and she poured bad scotch into the empty bottle of a fancier brand that had probably been someone's gift. She connected the lack of food to a bohemian spirit. It was also a way of getting revenge on her friends, the Communist Party members who treated her like she was bourgeois and mocked her aristocratic parlor. Like one nuclear physicist, born in Berlin and raised in Mexico, whose mother presided over the Eastern Writers' Union. The already minimal portions continued to diminish from year to year.

Faced with this anorexic drift, some of them started bringing food. Pierre Estenne, the surgeon-forger whom my grandparents always called by his prewar name, came with sauerkraut and liverwurst from his native Alsace. Alfred Szabados was a serious cook, and he spent hours in the kitchen, solemnly preparing a particularly hearty goulash.

They never talked about what, at the base of it, brought them together. The past was unspoken and full of ghosts. They erased duration. To speak their version of the unspeakable? To describe the home for refugees that had sheltered them? The wife and two children gassed? The arrest at the village school? Their experience with SS doctors in the Birkenau infirmary or the father propped against a wall and shot? How could they? They also didn't say much about what had followed, except for the calamities—the mathematician lover who suffocated with his mother because a coal stove malfunctioned. The commercial attaché who succumbed to bronchitis after he returned from the camps. The old, deported man who became depressive after a bad fall in a pool and ended up taking his own life. Deaths that were supposedly accidental, and therefore describable, though they clearly owed little to chance. Their chaotic double or triple lives weren't coincidences either—the string of their affairs, divorces, and secret children. The past only came up in anecdotal and meaningless ways or through roundabout routes.

Fred and Fritzi Brauner never stopped arguing over correct German grammar. He'd grown up in Vienna. She was born there. Part-time child psychologists and part-time teachers, they would arrive with an enormous projector and show us films they had made about groups of patients with autism and Down's syndrome. The work they did at their Saint-Mandé center was directly connected to their rescue of 426 child survivors of Buchenwald whom they housed in an old sanatorium after the liberation and those they had saved in Spain, through their work with the International Brigades eight years earlier. But they never talked about that earlier part of their life. Fred often played with Anne, my sister, Ariane, and me as if we were mice in his lab. He liked to get us worked up, to bring us out of our shells, but as soon as we started bouncing off the walls and yelling, he would call out to the adults in his singsong voice, "Perhaps you should calm them down a bit!"

She welcomed them standing up, very straight, leaning on an inlaid card table, so she could give the impression of being able bodied. Once the greetings were over, she would take her place in the middle of them and stay there, in her armchair, for the rest of the party, her limp legs like the limbs of a jointed doll, arranged next to each other on the edge of the velvet seat. Unruffled, she smiled and squinted at the smoke from a menthol Kool, a sugary-tasting cigarette, which she held with the tips of her fingers as if the filter were burning. Her spot in the center of the parlor was strengthened by her immobility. This colorful, flamboyant world revolved around her axis. They all came to her. As soon as she stood behind the ivory inlaid table, they bent in half to press the bony hand she lifted with a negligent air. Once she sat, they pulled their chairs up close to hers, trying to catch her attention, offering her one of the tiny sandwiches she refused with a pout. She ate nothing, only sipped a brown or yellow liqueur like Bailey's or Advocaat. She stayed close with all of them. They trusted her. She knew their secrets and they knew hers.

7

Her brother almost bumped the chandelier with his tall, gaunt body, his pointed head like a bird of prey's, and most of all his big, courtroom gestures. He was wearing a white shirt and a dark, threadbare suit, probably his only one, maybe the same one he'd worn twenty-five years earlier, at the peak of his brief political career, for his audience with president Réné Coty. He affected the air of someone who goes from one important meeting to another, as if he were still the head of the Territorial Assembly of the Austral Islands in French Polynesia. Bébé, his wife, came with him. He called all the women he lived with Bébé out of nonchalance and to avoid any mix-ups, since he housed more than one at a time. She was much younger than he was, and this was her first trip outside of the Polynesian archipelago.

Petite, with long, very straight black hair and a stocky, ageless body, she had trouble speaking French despite the many years she'd spent with him. Almost mute, she listened, nodded, and gazed up at him with approval. I never found out her real name. He told his sister intricate stories of trickery, of injustices he'd suffered years earlier, over there in Papeete, the capital of Tahiti, or on Tubuai, his lost paradise, the last island before the South Pole. To back up his tales, he carried dog-eared copies of papers with him. "Noël Ilari, former Captain of the Reserve Artillery, Volunteer Fighter at Verdun, in Poland, and the Loire, twice wounded, cited six times for valor, Former Chief of Youth Activities and Athletics in Tonkin . . ." This was his signature on the letters he wrote with his typewriter and sent to all kinds of authorities. It went on for a dozen lines. In his missives, he denounced nuclear testing, wrongdoing by local elected officials, the cultish nature of free masonry, the "maffia" which he spelled with two *f*s to underline its nefarious character. With distance, time contracted like a shift in perspective. He skipped whole eras without worrying about chronology, describing events that had happened a half century before with the same zeal, the same freshness as something that took place the day before. I can't remember anymore how he came to tell the story of his arrival in Vichy during the summer of 1940, his visits to the Hôtel du Parc, his society dinners at Chantecler, and his contribution to "national recovery." He talked about it without hesitation and didn't share the taboo of men from his generation who were overshadowed by the Gaullist myth of national resistance, as if by going far away, he'd hibernated all through those years. He was like the forgotten Japanese soldiers who were unaware that their country had surrendered and stayed holed up in the jungle with their old shotguns.

During Vichy, he never committed any crime punishable by

a court martial. As a member of Laval's first cabinet, he was an advisor to Jean Borotra, the former tennis player named minister of sports, a particularly coveted post that glorified strength and discipline. His role was limited to holding grand openings at stadiums and writing press releases. He had gotten the job through "a special friend," who, he let it be known, was also extremely generous in her favors to the prime minister. He certainly had the right profile for the task: a hypernationalist Catholic, raised by monks, an old member of the Croix du Feu and the Young Patriots, an admirer of powerful men. He liked Marshal Pétain and especially the emperor, whom he claimed as an ancestor through some vague relation (cousins?) between his great-grandmother Camilla Ilari and Napoleon Bonaparte, but really she had only been his nurse. For a while, he encouraged Napoleon's heir, the prince Louis, to claim his rights, and inundated him with phony letters of support, supposedly from every corner of the populace. Letters he signed on behalf of fake café proprietors, dressmakers, and delivery men in Les Halles. Aside from their shared ideology, he was eager to help Borotra so he could return to his lagoon in the Pacific as fast as possible, where he'd left a native woman and a son. He wanted to go back home, preferably in a position of power, so he could see his child, and more importantly get even with some policeman, a Chinese man, the governor, an elder from Papeete Lodge, and his thousands of other enemies, real or imaginary.

In 1934 he'd left everything—his job as an advisor, his handsome apartment near the Étoile, his "little capers" in Passy, his marriage that was blessed by the bishop, his upper-class spouse—all that for passage on an eighty-ton schooner, a rotting boat that nearly missed Tubuai and headed toward the pole. The reasons for his hurried departure remain mysterious. One escapade too many? An existential crisis? Gauginstyle fantasies, mixing paradise and a taste for very young women? In French Polynesia, he discovered concubines and slaves. Through some combination of paranoia, quixotism, and clairvoyance, he associated the local administration with the eternal "maffia" he pursued beyond the seas and with a colonial system built on forced labor and predatory loans. He ran afoul of the government from the moment he arrived in the archipelago, and his many commercial setbacks—he tried in vain to sell coffee—were followed by political ones. His endless fights, his duels with state-issued revolvers, his lawsuits served at the slightest offense, his rants that dragged on under the palm trees, his demonstrations on horseback—wearing dressage boots, linen riding jacket, and white gloves—made him the laughingstock of all Oceania when he managed to return to Tahiti in 1940 with his dreams of getting even and his written orders stamped with the insignia of Pétain's battle axe. He was too late. The Gaullists had just taken power. They wouldn't let him off the boat. Used to marching, chin up, at the battery, he was tempted to throw a punch. His Vichy superiors ordered him to Saigon to direct youth groups. He didn't return to his lagoon until the end of the war.

Mère-grand went to visit him in the midseventies and got one of her best novels out of the trip. *The Island of Sainte-Enfance* resembled Marguerite Duras in its languor and suffocation. Her brother lived there barricaded on his property, which he pompously called "The Hermitage of Sainte-Helena" in memory of Napoleon. In front was a large wooden board where he'd scrawled the word *Tabu*. Off limits. After he got routed in an election, he didn't want to see anyone and grumbled about his old constituents: "They took advantage of me. No matter what happens, I'll never be one of them." He'd fought for their independence, done time in prison, sacrificed every-thing for them, he repeated bitterly. He thought of himself once again as a captive in this far-flung corner of the world, which he finally realized wasn't his. He scraped by on a meager school-teacher's pension, surrounded by a few pieces of furniture from their family, which she recognized despite their wildly different context. She said that he re-created the Rennes apartment of their childhood in the tropics in both appearance and preten-sions—at once bourgeois and penniless. Seeing him eat in the kitchen for lack of household help or hide to avoid the neigh-bors, she was reminded of her father, their father, that other broken man in poor health who spent whole days slumped in his green armchair. Same tatty wool jacket, same laughable efforts to pretend things had ended up differently. The only thing he cared about was his legacy. On the road encircling the lagoon, which had no other notable landmarks, rare tour-ists photographed his monument, the only one on the island. A tomb he'd built in the middle of his property, after a last judicial battle with the administration. His own Saint-Helena memorial. Mosaic fragments of dark seashells spelled out his Corsican name. Only the date was missing. The epitaph was already engraved: "He died faithful to his God, his family, his ideas, and his ungrateful country, after long years of moral ag-ony in the isolation and solitude of this place." This was his last letter of protest.

8

She found herself straddling a rift, a seismic zone, something collapsing where two opposing worlds met—the one she had chosen and the one that rejected her. Her friends were all survivors. Jews with fuzzy identities, Communists who would soon be adrift, gay men entrenched in the sanctuary of Saint-Germain-des-Prés. Pariahs, despite their bourgeois way of life. People who were brilliant but broken, shipwrecks with no bearings, delivered from all attachments, animated by a sharp feeling of precariousness. Their sense of the relative, their understanding of the fragility of the social order made them freer, more open, more indulgent despite their lives marked by death.

Her family was trapped in an unescapable tangle of pretense, conventions, codes to respect, rank to uphold. The mother with a fancy name who reserved her greetings in the street for the right people and turned her face away from others; the father a penniless lawyer decorated by the Vatican with the order of Saint-Gregory and addicted to morphine. Each time he ran short, furious and desperate, he would send his reputation-conscious spouse all over Rennes begging for doses from more and more reluctant apothecaries. Her brother, descended from the Marquis d'Ilari, Napoleon I, the kings of Tubuai and who knows what else, whose fate never measured up to his delusions of grandeur. Their maid, because one was required, whose wages were negotiated to almost nothing through her orphanage but who was always unhappy with her lot and never stayed long. The Carmelite sister, the one who went crazy after falling in love with a priest, and the third sister, the iconic one, papa's "little saint" Thérèse de Lisieux, a close likeness given what a wildflower she was. They belonged—of course—to a completely different world. The world of the right, flag waving, traditional, antirepublican, deeply marked by the social doctrine of the church, and rife with an old, anti-Semitic Christianity. Some of them cooperated a little too much with the invaders. Her entourage belonged to the present. But her family was turned to the past.

9

She was the seventh. Madeleine, Suzanne, Marie-Thérèse, Anne, Noël, Adrienne. One birth a year. And finally, her, Marie-Élise, the littlest one. The child the confessor pushed for, urging the exhausted mother to resume her conjugal duties after every pregnancy. An unbearable burden. One more girl. One more dowry or convent to find. Most of all, another mouth to feed in a family reduced, according to one story worthy of a saint's tale, to eating wafer crumbs, which tasted like cardboard pieces of a puzzle, and cracked wheat, which they could buy for almost nothing at the bakers. No space for her in that family who never set foot outside on the first of January for fear of running into the concierge and having to give her a tip.

At her baptism, her father, Adrien, wept. Did he already know that they weren't celebrating a rite of passage but a hand-off? He had found her much more than a simple godmother—a tutor, a wealthy widow who was ready to raise Marie-Élise and leave her an inheritance when she died. He waited until she was old enough to go to school and to perceive what was happening to her but still too young to understand why she was given to her benefactress. She was torn from her family, from the room she shared with her sisters, from the town with granite walls, from everything she recognized, even the name that was given to her before the altar. Her adoptive mother rebaptized her, as if she were a new pet. Marie-Élise became Myriam. The fashion in Brittany was for Biblical first names. From then on, she was her daughter. Her companion girl. She found herself in the woman's service. On the baptismal font, they had sold her to a single woman who lived a secluded life and heaped lessons on her, sermons sprinkled with shriveled, shallow kisses.

By her childhood logic, she must have done something wrong. Too meek to imagine herself as naughty, she believed she'd been kicked out for her ugly face. Her parents told her she looked like grandmother Flora, the long-ago *mammone* from Corsica, with her black mane and huge eyes, strange features that weren't from there, not part of that great, humid West. She went back to see them for two weeks a year. Brief visits, arranged in the contract. The only father she knew spent his days sitting, a cap on his head, poking the red coals as if he were always cold, in his filthy apartment on the Vilaine, full of patched curtains and linens but not a single molding missing. He didn't practice anymore, except for one or two clients sent by a solicitor. "Oh little Lise, you came too late," her sisters would tell her. "He's only a shadow of his former self." They would fill her head with memories of his glory days, which sounded to her like fairy stories. The youngest president of the French bar, defender of the church, recognized by the pope after his trials during the Inventory Quarrels. But he was already poor, preferring grand causes to large sums. Even lost causes. With his son Noël, he shared a taste for solitary, desperate fights, a propensity to feel misunderstood, unloved, an attraction to the tragic, a melodramatic side, traits that, in this part of France, at the very bottom of the map, probably encouraged a family saga peppered with heroic acts, vendettas, and crimes of honor.

The injections he shouted for—were they the cause or the consequence of his decline? As a parliamentary candidate for the first district of Saint-Nazaire, he never got over his defeat to a close friend of Aristide Briand's. A disappointment that was exacerbated by early results that would have made him the winner. When a tie was announced later that night, he cried fraud and was defeated in the runoff a week later. He also owed his failure to his shaky position on the political chessboard of the era. "Social because Catholic," his materials proclaimed. Too social for the Right. Too religious for the Left. He lost on both fronts. Afterward, everything fell apart. He started to complain of sciatica. Intense bouts called for opiates in higher and higher doses. His addiction, which literature associates with debauchery, certainly ended up ensuring it. All of good Rennes society must have looked down on this ruined man who almost never left the house. Each time she visited, his daughter saw him suffer more, trembling with anger, then begging that they put an end to this cross he had to bear. She watched on the stairs as her mother ran out to get the vials, most often returning empty handed, red with shame from the pharmacist's reproach. Unless she succeeded in convincing the man, in which case the terrified child helped with the ritual. The case, never cleaned, an old Pravaz silver syringe, the enormous, worn needle, the arm scribbled with mysterious tattoos, the sweating face, which relaxed all at once, and finally, the office door closing, the "Shh! He's sleeping," murmured by the oldest sister, her finger to her lips.

10

On the mantel in the parlor, she kept a black marble clock from her father, which she compared to a gravestone or to a stele in memory of her scheduled trips to see him, to visit his bedside. In my time, the mechanism didn't work anymore. No one thought of repairing or simply winding it, as if it bore witness to a denial of time's passing, a widespread attitude at the Rue-de-Grenelle, or to a life left sleeping. When, in spite of its faulty machinery, the object was stolen in the late seventies, my grandmother didn't seem particularly upset. She wasn't very interested in material things and her relationships with the

Ilari were complicated. Their mutual incomprehension caused a stalemate. She resented them. They'd been neglectful. They envied her. For her dresses as a little girl and, as an adult, for everything they'd been denied: money, freedom, independence. She reproached them for her solitude. They had abandoned her, handed her over to others out of concern for propriety. They didn't understand her anger. They thought they had suffered more. She was revolted by the prejudices of their class, by their hypocrisies dressed up as virtues. Since they'd thrown her out, it was even easier to reject the familial order they represented. She was a rebel. They saw her as an heiress.

11

As she got older, she went less and less often to visit the lands she'd inherited. She left in the morning and tried to come back the same night despite the five- or six-hour drive. Highways, endless routes bordered with trees and full of trucks. It was usually raining. We were rocked to sleep by the regular batting of the windshield wipers. Toward the end, we drove through desolate villages, their slate roofs running with water. Jean-Élie took the wheel. Sitting next to him, she slept and didn't wake up until we saw the gray steeple of Désertines. She hated this humid Mayenne—sad, cold, and muddy—where she'd spent a part of her youth. She'd do anything to avoid spending the night at the "chateau," as the villagers called it, emphasizing the *o* in the last syllable, a vast dwelling covered in ivy, which hadn't been touched since her godmother's death. Unheated, without facilities, smelling of wet wood and moldy upholstery. Two big black pines planted on either side of the house plunged it into a perpetual dusk. A cemetery stretched out at the end of the garden. She had to climb over a stone porch. As soon as she arrived, she transformed into an old-fashioned feudal overlord.

Without taking off her coat, she sat in the great hall on the ground floor, in one of the red velvet chairs. A clay pot on the table held freshly cut dahlias. A meal was cooling in the kitchen, always the same one: milk and onion soup followed by roast pork and potatoes. Once lunch was over, she gathered her people, with her fur around her shoulders. Farmers, housekeepers, notaries queued up in a room that remained freezing despite a fire in the hearth. They held their caps in their hands and came with their bills and their grievances. In a hurry to get back to Paris, she listened to them with barely concealed impatience.

12

Once a month, she hosted gatherings for her cell in her Louis-the-something-or-other style parlor. Her subscribers to the Sunday *L'Humanité* were all there. The evenings produced more social ceremony than preparation for a Soviet takeover of the Winter Palace. The poet talked about his health problems and his dear, departed muse. The banker from the USSR never mentioned money much less the impenetrable twists and turns of international finance. "We lost a battle, but we haven't lost the war," an editor repeated after every defeat. A militant woman talked about Russia like one of her old friends. "She didn't know. She wasn't informed," she said; "They didn't tell her what was happening." Most of all, there was the question of manning a booth, the lilies of the valley, the pins or stamps to sell, newspapers to deliver, chores that everyone tried to get out of while still being very courteous and displaying enthusiasm. What was she doing there? There were always two sides to her. Both landowner and card-carrying Communist, excluded and elected, adopted and advantaged, handicapped and globe-trotting, powerless and omnipotent, grandmother and Big Bad Wolf.

Staircase

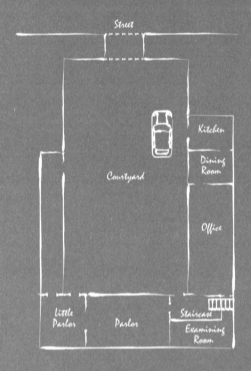

Street

Kitchen

Dining Room

Courtyard

Office

Little Parlor

Parlor

Staircase

Examining Room

1

She wove between obstacles, following a fixed choreography. Always with Anne and Jean-Élie by her side, held by the vise of their arms, in the pincer of their bodies. The repetitive nature of her gestures, their slowness, my aunt and uncle's gravity as they helped her walk, gave each of her movements a solemn air, like a procession. Despite her limping gait, she resembled a queen, parading around her rooms at the appointed hour, in the company of her court. Her entrance was announced by creaking doors, sounds of furniture moving, and the irregular clacking of her heels on the parquet. It took tremendous energy to get from one floor to another. She groped along the staircase with her birdlike claws, gripping the metal bannister that hugged the rounded wall, counteracting her paralyzed legs with the strength of her arms and her fists, raising her pelvis to lift a foot, placing it on the step, pressing on it as if it were a wooden pillar, making her second leg pivot, throwing it forward, her face tight, leaning all her weight on her children, and slowly beginning to climb with the fearful majesty of the disabled.

Two to four times a day, sometimes more, she fought this same battle. Nine feet of elevation to traverse, two landings without anything to hold on to, and, at the turn, dangerous blade-shaped steps. Before her ordeal, she assumed the stance of a champion before a match. She cocked her head to gauge the distances, stuck out her tongue, flexed her muscles, at least the ones that hadn't been ravaged by polio, muscles healthy people don't notice, hidden in folds, at the joints of limbs. Her whole amputated self was held out toward some invisible point a long way in front of her. Suddenly, with a little "ahan!" of anger, she'd become aggressive, as if she were going into combat. There was a part of herself she still couldn't master, and she fought it like she fought everything around her: grooves, strips, boards, bars, abysses, hollows, handles, elbows. Once in motion, she divided objects and subjects into two inevitable camps: the allies she could lean on and the more numerous enemies that obstructed or betrayed her, an all-or-nothing kind of judgment. In this binary space, I belonged to the second category. During her descent or climb, I had to be out of sight. I was too little to help her. I risked hindering or bumping her or worse—witnessing a bad fall, a stumble, a humiliating contortion. At any moment, she could find herself on the ground, reduced to a pile of rags. I didn't have a right to be there. If I lingered on the landing, she would say to her bearers, in a voice loud enough to carry, "I don't want him here!"

2

When the godmother presented her to the ladies in town, she was scrubbed, dressed in one of her newly acquired frocks, decked out in ribbons like an Easter egg. The woman explained, during a five-o'clock tea, that she had chosen the girl carefully, after getting all the necessary information from the right people who knew the family and its genetic flaws. "There are so many unpleasant surprises with unknown heredity," they told her. The godmother's guests complimented her on her choice as they nibbled little cakes. They gushed over the girl's thick hair, her big, sad eyes, but they had the politeness not to mention her almost pygmy size. Marie Nélet was proud of her latest acquisition, which she evaluated with a trainer's eye. She needed to think about what tricks to teach her. She called the girl her "little negress" because of her curls and took her self-effacing manners for a blank page on which she could make her mark.

She collected children like other people collect trophies. In her youth, she had been attracted by the monastic life. Married off to a judge, she'd wanted to be a mother. As a widow with no descendants, perhaps unable to have children, she'd become a teacher. In Fougères she ran a charity house in one of her father's old mills. A "big open cage," as she put it, where she kept her poor little girls to rescue them—I'm quoting her again—from the "horrors of the street." She plucked them out of the rural proletariat, mostly female, who worked in the many shoe factories in town. Her teachings, which were delivered in the evenings or during holidays, consisted of catechism and needlework. She prepared them not so much to accomplish as to accept the only destiny available—piety and boot making. Prayers, rosaries, clouds of incense, and sewing needles were her typical pedagogical tools. She was on a mission. She answered the call of her pope, who had just discovered social welfare. She battled both the misery of the working woman and those who, in her eyes, exploited this type; really, these were her direct competition, the "abusers of the ideal," the "agitators," the "foreigners" who riled up the crowds and turned her protégées away from the immaculate path she had laid out for them. During the big strike in the winter of 1906, she was upset to see several of her students, the same ones she'd sent a few months earlier to recite the Paternoster among the mutineers.

She had six other goddaughters that people brought to her on holidays, dressed up like princesses to demonstrate the good use of her money. She showered them in generosity and homilies but only intended her fortune for Marie-Élise, or rather Myriam. "They gave you to me for your own good," she kept telling her—"You'll understand later on." My grandmother never really understood. Her sisters before God, their families, the household staff, the five-o'clock tea ladies all asked the same question—why her? They surveyed this sickly heiress with a mixture of pity and envy, wondering what her mother-in-spirit could see in her. "In the future, all this will be yours," they told her in a greedy tone. They all looked at her as if she were both at the bottom of the ladder and the top of the stairs. She had no wish to rise through the ranks they gave her. She had to keep herself from screaming at them. No, she was not from the gutter. She had a family, a name. She wasn't a bastard, a Cinderella, or a girl from nothing, and even less a gold digger. And she'd never asked anyone for anything.

3

Rue-de-Grenelle wasn't unlike those Mediterranean dwellings that include rooms for appearance, accessible to visitors, open to the exterior or a courtyard, and private bedrooms and bathrooms, gynaeceums reserved for women and children, secluded or upstairs. The higher you went into the building, the more intimate it became (*intimate*, which comes from Latin, *intimus*, the superlative form of the adjective *interior*, which means "within"). More literally, the intimate means what is contained in the deepest space of a being. Or of a place. The second floor was my grandmother's domain. To get to her rooms, she passed the "derrières," as they called them in Louis XIV's court, the chambers reserved for the family. She never used the other possible route—a little platform followed by a few steps that linked her bedroom to the staircase—because that barren space was devoid of handholds. We called it, dismissively, "the landing," which implies a break between two inclines, but in this case it was really a stoop.

I'd taken over this no-man's-land that my grandfather also abandoned for its impracticality. I used to sit on the steps and make up stories with my toy soldiers, using here and there the ledges of the stairs as a game board. It was an ideal observation post, allowing me to keep an eye on everything that went on in the courtyard and the house. The one wall of the staircase, opposite the window, was pierced by an opaque porthole. On the left side, there was a painting. The canvas reminded me of a Magritte. It showed a big head, very round, wearing a bowler hat, which mirrored the blind bull's-eye of glass. I think it was called "Young Englishman." When you came in through the foyer, the first thing you saw was this watcher with a fixed, mysterious gaze. I imagined he protected us from thieves.

4

Outside of her pedagogical activities, Marie Nélet wrote novels under the name Myriam Thélen. Works full of religion and feminism. They've never been reprinted, but used copies of them are for sale online. Especially *At Dawn*, published in 1905 by Perrin. As soon as I received the book in the mail, I found an inscription in her handwriting in turquoise ink: "I dedicate this book to the father and mother of three handsome little apostles, Philippe, Jean, and Pierre, so that it may speak to them about Jesus's country and communicate this author's dear friendship." Her work was intended for souls, and preferably young ones, rather than readers. *At Dawn* does indeed take place in Judea during King Herod's time. It was part of a whole educational literature of toga-clad dramas in fashion at the end of the nineteenth century after the worldwide success of *Ben Hur* by Lewis Wallace and *Quo Vadis* by the Polish writer

Henryk Sienkiewicz. Her book, very roughly summarized, is the story of a woman oppressed by her father, a shepherd in Hebron, then forced to marry a fickle husband; a woman who, in the prime of life, succeeds in getting her freedom through knowledge, work, and of course a budding faith in Christ. The roughly woven narrative, the hokey plot, the overblown style, and the many quotes taken from the Old and New Testaments make it hard to read today. I understand why my grandmother never mentioned it.

In flipping through, I recalled a series of sepia images of palm trees, camels, peasants in headscarves, people in long priest's robes. At Désertines, there were hundreds of them printed on glass plates. Photos that were mounted in duplicate, overlapping but slightly off kilter, to create an illusion of depth. I would look inside a big mahogany box, pressing my eyes to a pair of lenses. A mirror at the top of the apparatus caught the ambient light. Golden buttons on the sides let you adjust the focus. The stereoscope was varnished with the patina of an old violin and placed on a little windowsill where you could just glimpse the village bell tower. The photos had been taken by the godmother during her pilgrimage to the Holy Land, an obligatory rite of passage for any Catholic writer. Ever since this voyage, which she undertook at the turn of the century in the company of a young Assumptionist, she cultivated a passion for an unchanging and biblical Orient. Hence the choice of Myriam, the Hebrew version of Mary, the mother of Jesus, or the name of the prophetess, sister of Moses and Aaron. She used it as a new first name for her girl but also as her pen name, authoring her two biggest works under the same pseudonym.

5

Mem, resh, yud, mem. Myriam. She liked to stick her name on her most valuable possessions. The four Hebrew letters were engraved on each of the books the godmother left her. Handsome volumes bound in leather by an artisan in Fougères, with marbled paper and golden edges. When I was a child they filled the glass cabinet in the vestibule at the bottom of the stairs. Later they were repatriated to the office. Or more likely, forgotten. They were mostly novels or travel books. *The Fear of Living* by Henri Bordeaux. *The Virgins of the Rocks* by Gabriele D'Annunzio. *Syria, Palestine, Mount Athos* and *The Dead Who Speak* by Eugène-Melchior de Vogüé. *Spanish Soil* by René Bazin. *The Conquest of Jerusalem* by Myriam Harry, which won the first Prix Femina. Writers who were, for the most part, monarchists, social Catholics, or nationalists. There was also *The Jewish Soul* by father Stéphen Coubé, a preacher at the Madeleine who was famous for his rages against the God killers. An anti-Semitic harangue dedicated, like the others, to "Myriam Thélen."

6

The girl was ashamed of her guardian, of her overly high-pitched voice, her too-big hat, of the way she acted like an eccentric grande dame, shouting at her on the bus, "Myriam! Did you wash behind your ears?" In her presence, the girl shrank. She forced herself to disappear. She had to be good, to avoid making noise. In her own way, her benefactress loved her. She simply didn't know how to take care of a child. Despite her mothering role, she maintained the habits of a widow. She demanded quiet, had dinner early, ate little. She had few guests and scorned the ungenerous spirit of small towns. More and more often, she went to Paris, where she enjoyed a certain notoriety as a novelist. She was an active member of the Society of Letters. One of her books—*The Messenger*, a story of her experience as a teacher in Fougères—had received a prize from the Académie française. A singular woman, caught between her feminist aspirations, her literary ambitions, and her bigotry. She was massive, round faced, red skinned. She dressed badly. Everything about her was frumpy. The little girl called her *mémé*. A name that, said fast enough, could be confused with *maman*. So that once, waking from a nightmare and crying out for her biological mother, her godmother came running, thinking she'd been called. Their relationship was based on a misunderstanding.

7

She never said she had polio. When people asked about her handicap, she replied: "I took a fall!" as if she'd come back from skiing with a sprain. Until the end, she refused even the subtlest orthopedic assistance. It seemed unbearable to her that a pair of crutches would attract others' attention, and even worse, their pity. No question of using a wheelchair at the airport either—a service freely offered to people with even slightly reduced mobility. The day before any such feat, she would get ready. In 1974, as soon as Roissy-Charles-de-Gaulle airport rose up from the beet and grain fields of French soil, she started studying the entrances to the gates, spread out in a star around the wheel, the "camembert." To avoid slipping on endless escalators of the central lounge, she would go to Montparnasse-Bienvenüe on Sunday mornings to practice on the moving walkways, the longest ones in the Paris subway system. She trained like an athlete, performing multiple crossings back and forth. She put particular effort into hopping on and off the ends of the conveyor. The hardest part was to jump just as the belt started to turn. She wanted to go unnoticed, to lead a normal life. At Rue-de-Grenelle, she could have arranged the interior to aid her comings and goings, but it was unthinkable for her to turn the house into a hospital. It wasn't until the very end that she had a dumbwaiter installed, in a spot she probably wanted to destroy. That might have been the whole point of the undertaking. But more on this later.

She thought she was just like other people. She was feminine, attentive to her appearance, well groomed, liking to please, to go out, to travel. Inside her, everything worked. Her mind galloped. She radiated energy. She couldn't hold still. She floundered, not like a wounded animal, but like a fawn caught in a snare. She was only an invalid in the eyes of the healthy. As soon as they noticed her halting steps, she was nothing more than that, a crippled woman people tried to help, offering their arms, holding doors modestly, with a look that was full of kindliness. For all those people, she was nothing but an excuse for some generous act, which she would greet with a flurry of insults, since she still preferred revulsion to mercy. The sudden fear she inspired at least made her equal. She refused to be shut up in a box. She just had a problem with coordination. When she told her legs to move, they no longer obeyed her orders or followed them shoddily and late. This obstacle annoyed her in daily life but didn't make her someone "different."

Buying shoes required a long expedition with the family as usual. She always bought them from Alice Nuchi's mother, at her Swiss Village store, which was so tight and crowded it looked like a storage room. Mère-grand would try on dozens of pairs before selecting the right one, usually pumps with pointed toes and square heels. She winced as she looked in the mirror at her tiny feet, floating in a sea of crinkled paper. To ease her worry about showing her physical constraints, she opened nearly all the boxes in the shop. Considering her handicap, she should have chosen flat ankle boots with support, but she wanted to be a few inches taller, elegant, and most importantly, to look like other women. Once she bought the shoes, she brought them to a cobbler to get them shaved down. The craftsman lived far away, in the suburbs. She'd gone to a lot of trouble finding him. In order to correct something, maybe a warp in the arch of her foot, the man had to sand off the end of each heel into a gentle slope. She watched him shape the wood into a beveled edge. She would take a few steps, a kind of test, and leave with her lopsided shoes. It was patched together. Everything was fine as long as she could avoid podiatrists and specialty stores.

8

As a teenager, she revolted. In *Found Parents*, she recounts an escape followed by a long discussion. She announced that she couldn't stand any more sermons in church, any more love as an annuity, tenderness on command. She apologized for not being a good placement and declared that she was closing her accounts. Terminating her contract through the abuse clause. Marie Nélet listened. Maybe for the first time. Once the tirade was over, she said, "Get dressed, my dear, we'll go out to eat and we'll talk it over calmly."

She hadn't known how to be a mother, so she got to work

becoming a friend. She took Myriam to Italy. Rome, the Vatican, the catacombs, Saint Paul's tomb. For her, tourism and pilgrimage were one and the same. The young lady scorned religious trinkets, didn't pay any attention to the fascist parades—Mussolini had just come into power—and discovered the effect she had on boys. She loved her trip. She and her chaperone developed an understanding. She pardoned the lady preacher and learned to respect the suffragette. Myriam began to see her godmother as a liberator who, after buying her, would set her free. Her sisters lived in poverty, under the yoke of a Corsican father who, during the First World War, threatened to kill them to preserve their honor if the "Teutons" got as far as Rennes. She was free. Soon, she would be rich. Above all, she understood that her godmother loved her: "My happiness was the biggest, maybe the only, point of her life," she wrote.

She began studying medicine, presumably though her godmother's influence. A few years earlier Marie Nélet had published *The Intern* with Dr. Marthe Bertheaune, another pseudonym. A partly autobiographical tale. Her coauthor was one of the first women in France to pass the hospital intern exam. Anne Darcanne-Mouroux, to call her by her real name, was a pioneer and a gynecologist. She directed a clinic in Fougères. She wanted to liberate women's bodies, starting with physical fitness, and was the head of a society for women's sports. She and her husband lived apart. To those who were shocked by his absence, she always gave the same answer: "He's gone hunting!" she would say, without specifying the nature of his prey. Marie Nélet initiated her into literature and then into Parisian life. They were inseparable, cosigning another novel called *Doctor Odile*. Later on, Dr. Anne wrote several novels, intended as examples, for the "young women and young girls" collection at Fayard. Her heroines, confronted with difficult dilemmas, always chose to put duty before their feelings. My grandmother couldn't stand Dr. Anne, but she followed in her footsteps.

9

After a childhood like hers, it's understandable that she relentlessly tried to re-create what she had been denied: a family conceived as a solid block. She didn't go anywhere without her people around her. "My children are my canes," she would say. It was obviously a method designed to keep herself upright and to keep us close. Her children stayed attached, handcuffed to her. In reach, everywhere, at all times. Jean-Élie on the right, Anne to the left. And behind them, one of her other children. "For a very long time, my arm was always bent, ready to help her," Christian says, and it occurs to him to wonder if she didn't exaggerate her difficulty to better maintain her power over us. Sometimes it was my turn to be her brace. I felt her pincers closing on my fingers, her skeleton straightening, her entire weight leaning on me. She was the only one who kept us almost constantly aware of her own body. We were her missing limbs, her stepstools, or her moving supports, like the chairs she pushed in front of her. Maybe there was no difference between us and these inanimate objects, these surroundings. We were part of the furniture.

10

How and where did she meet him? In the lecture hall during one of his presentations on "cancers of the colon" or on "the treatment of abdominal adhesions and perivisceritis"? In a café, on the terrace of the Bullier? In a corridor of the Hôtel-Dieu? Was she part of the crowd of interns and nurses who followed him, step-by-step, between the iron cots and the stretchers? Or was it through the mediation of Zina, her accomplice from her first days of medical school? He was the department head, decorated with his gold intern's medal. She must have been in her second or third year of courses. They were alike. They both looked at the world with incomprehension. She was seduced by his olive skin, his wavy black hair, his little pointed moustache, and by the gentleness, the humanity with which he treated his patients. Unlike many of his eminent peers, he never seemed indifferent in the face of suffering. He fell for the charming young woman, twenty years old and without attachments and prejudices. By law, she hadn't reached the age of majority, but she no longer had a guardian to report to. Marie Nélet had recently died. She could accept anyone she wanted—there was no one to oppose it. Certainly not her biological family, who, in abandoning her, had ceded any rights. Only her father might have disagreed with her choice, but he was also dead.

Dr. Anne Darcanne-Mouroux met with them and gave her blessing. They were married July 10, 1929, at Désertines, on the lands that she'd just inherited. She was still dressed in mourning for her adoptive mother. The ceremony took place at night, almost on the sly, out of respect for the deceased. Or was it out of discretion? To avoid an uproar? Slander tends to dissolve in the dark. With the exception of the patriarch, all the Ilari were there, including the cousins. On the Boltanski side, there was only Étienne and his mother.

Niania arrived with her accent, her fake name, and an officer with a loud voice who waited on her gallantly. In the village square, everyone was talking about her "bad manners," her "vulgar lover." By the end of the day, scandal erupted at the town hall with the presentation of documents. On paper, she wasn't called Hélène Macagon but Enta Fainstein. She claimed to be Russian, but in the eyes of her future in-laws, she was nothing but a Jew. People shouted about stolen identity, trickery. She explained that in her country, people were chosen for mandatory military service by lottery. To avoid conscription, one of her Macagon ancestors changed his name with a boy who had been spared by luck, a certain Fainstein. Her confused story, told in bad pidgin French, didn't fool anyone.

Before the mayor, Myriam was flanked by Madeleine, her oldest sister. Étienne's witness was a certain Dr. Georges Lebedinsky. Like the mysterious medical student Lebedinsky who, thirty years earlier, attested Étienne's birth before a city hall official. This one was named Jacques. Was he the same man? Or was it another clerical error? Online, there's a Georges Lebedinsky who "died for France" in 1944 at Buchenwald, age twenty-two, the son of a Jacques Lebedinsky who died before the Second World War.

It must have been nearly ten at night before the couple emerged from the church. They took a carriage back to the great house under the pine trees, where a reception awaited them. In the great hall, lit by a petrol lamp, a dozen farmers in their Sunday best welcomed this circumcised son of the Batignolles with a shout: "Long live our new master!"

11

Twice a day, Jean-Élie rushed back down the stairs. He went down to the cellar to put coal in the central furnace. Each time he woke the fat, helpless monster balanced on its iron posts, the walls began to tremble. The sound of the shovel, the coals that banged against each other, and the crank my uncle turned with a forceful hand to make the ashes fall through the grille—all these noises rose through the pipes and echoed on every floor. Rue-de-Grenelle was a living being. I'm using the past tense, since the house has now returned to the stillness of a building. In my grandmother's day, it was made up of organs. The kitchen was the orifice. The brain's ghostly glow illuminated the office. The parlor was the skin. In this cameral anatomy, the stairs were the legs. We were swallowed in the belly of the whale. The philosopher Thomas Hobbes defined the leviathan as the antithesis of savagery, like an absolute authority, capable of establishing political order, of making peace and security reign. We'd taken refuge in limbo to escape the chaos outside.

12

It all started with a high fever, a terrible headache, a stiffness in her neck like a spasm, chills that went deep into her bones, as if her spine was turning into a block of ice. She thought she had the flu, had simply caught cold, despite the hot summer. The next day she fell down trying to get to the bathroom, as if she had chains around her ankles. Her teeth wouldn't stop chattering. She covered herself with hot-water bottles that gurgled under her Scottish plaid blanket. In the next few days, she got worse. Nausea, vomiting, intense tiredness, and horrible pain in her legs, especially the right. Impossible to get out of bed or even move. Lying motionless on her damp sheets, she cried like a little girl. The paralysis reached her left arm. A doctor tapped her sluggish knees with a mallet and diagnosed a case of acute anterior poliomyelitis. She was put in a contagious disease ward, isolated, intubated, placed under observation. At the end of the week, her temperature dropped sharply. She looked at her body crumpled on the mattress. It didn't look different, but it didn't obey her any more. Her limbs felt detached.

She escaped asphyxiation and slowly regained the use of her arm. Without a cure, she underwent "brand-new" shock therapy treatments, endless sessions to stretch her muscles five or six times a day, hot compresses on her arms and legs, surgeries that left her wrapped in plaster for months. She wanted to flee the hospital, that theater of passion. The "goners" the staff had stopped wasting time on, their beds empty in the early morning, their sheets tightly fitted, without the slightest wrinkle, and around them, the constant dance of orderlies and nurses. The boss, followed by his court, who offered his verdict from the foot of the iron cot without a spare glance at the accused. As soon as they were stretched out, human beings were attended to like sliced-open mice, ready to be dissected. A general silence discouraged questions from patients and those close to them. She already knew this. It was only that she had passed from the stage to an orchestra seat. She started to hate the show. Until the end of her life, she abhorred medicine and those who served it. She rebelled against sickness, against the healthy, against everyone who wanted to keep her in her new state.

13

Saturdays and Sundays, the days when grand-papa usually wasn't receiving patients, Anne, Ariane, and I turned the staircase into a sledding hill. We plummeted down the slope made by placing two foam mattresses end to end. Big pillows were our luges. At the turn, we stuffed blankets into the gap between the beds. Usually, the rough wool slowed our descent and we ended up stuck in the curve of the wall. Jean-Élie was always afraid we would hurt ourselves. He was particularly worried we would get our heads caught between the metal spokes of the bannister, a highly unlikely hypothesis considering the size of our skulls, but he couldn't stop thinking about it. We also liked to pull ourselves back up the slope, still seated on our bolsters, using the strength of our grip. As soon as we let go, we would slide back down. We always headed right back to the summit. All children like to play Sisyphus. But were we also trying to imitate mère-grand as she pushed her boulder?

14

How did she catch it? The virus enters though the mouth, breeds in the lymph nodes of the neck, and then reaches the nervous system. Its transmission is almost exclusively between people and most often happens by way of dirty water or food contaminated with feces. Back then, no one knew how it spread, so everything was suspect. She blamed her husband. When she found out that he'd had affairs before their marriage, which wasn't surprising considering the age difference (he was twelve years older), she'd thrown a fit and fallen ill shortly after. She thought her polio came from nervous shock. Then she accused the stagnant water in the lower lake of the Bois du Boulogne, which she'd carelessly swallowed in the course of a boat ride. During each epidemic, doctors told people not to drink from public fountains. She was most likely infected during her work at the hospital. She never finished medical school.

In a few months, she gained sixty pounds. She'd become deformed and risked being confined to her bed like the morbidly obese. She wanted to kill herself, but how could she do it without help? Étienne explained to her that the woman he loved was, in his eyes, intact, that normality doesn't exist, and that a human being can't be reduced to appendages. She lost weight, relearned how to walk with wooden crutches, which she loathed and nicknamed her "little undertakers." Everything

underfoot became dangerous and hostile. At the cost of countless falls and contortions, she learned to climb mountains,
plumb the depths of canyons, and even developed all kinds of
strategies to conceal her handicap. Any time she fell, she was
stuck, stretched on the ground, unable to lift herself up, waiting
hours for a helping hand. She couldn't be alone any more. She
had lost her hard-won independence and regained her childhood fear of abandonment. The sight of people running down
the street, hopping on a double-decker bus, or scrambling toward the mouth of a metro station left her inconsolable. She
looked around for the others, the unwell. In Paris after World
War I, she had no trouble finding them. She counted the mutilated as she had once counted handsome boys.

15

At the beginning of 1944, Luc was climbing the stairs alone.
Reaching the landing, he saw, through the door frame, the
curtains parting. Two feet appeared below the tulle. He ran
back downstairs shouting that he'd seen a ghost. His mother
went pale. She waited a few minutes before sending him back
upstairs. He climbed the steps one by one, nervous. Once he
reached the top, he found his older brother Jean-Élie in their
father's dressing gown, hiding behind the white fabric. "You
were trying to scare me!" the child cried, laughing.

Apartment

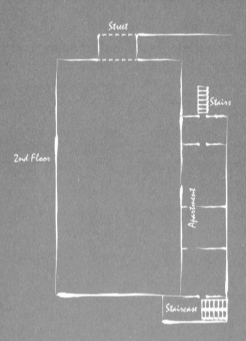

1

On the second floor, the right-hand door is unused. On the other side, Anne, my aunt, lives in a separate two-room apartment with a kitchen and bathroom. She gets to it by the common staircase, which opens onto the courtyard. She is four and a half years older than I am, and I think of her as a sister. Back then, she didn't live there. She had a child's bedroom next to the one mère-grand and grand-papa shared. When she babysat me, we would sometimes spend whole afternoons confined in her little niche in the heart of the house. We imagined that we were lost in the middle of an ocean. To escape the flood, we climbed onto her raised bed. From there, we jumped across to the hearth of the fireplace, then on to a trestle table. A ladder thrown across a chair allowed us to get back to our starting point. The game was to circle the room without ever touching the ground. We also played darts. We threw our projectiles wherever. I have one of Christian's paintings that hung over the fireplace, the first he had ever finished, and it bears some scars. We could do pretty much anything we wanted without getting the slightest scolding. In those days, she wasn't called Anne but Françoise. At the local school, she had a last name that sounded Spanish: Fondevilla. But I didn't know that.

When I was seven or eight years old, I learned that she wasn't my biological aunt. My other grandmother, Mamie, announced it one morning, bluntly, in her old school mistress's voice. "Françoise? She's adopted!" When I tried to deny it, her voice became hard. Almost sarcastic. As if she'd just uncovered a fraud and was mocking my belief. "Really? You didn't know? Nobody told you?" I thought they had hidden something shameful from me. Worse, I thought they would take my aunt, my big sister, away—that they would rip me from a part of myself. I burst into sobs. I remember crying for hours on the couch in her living room in Poissy while she told me, in her martial, Third Republic voice, to stop this "cinema."

Afterward, or maybe even before this discovery, I had the feeling of being taken in by the Rue-de-Grenelle. "If you want to go out, leave me at the Bolts" was apparently one of the first coherent sentences I pronounced in front of my parents. For a long time, I identified with Françoise. Around the same time, she and I arrived at "the Bolts," that pet name for the family kibbutz that sounded like an electric shock. She was still a very little girl, and I was a baby.

When Myriam decided to adopt, was she trying to find her orphan double? To copy her godmother's gesture? To create a new lineage not founded on blood but on choice? Or did she want to fill some emptiness? A few months earlier, my father Luc had committed the unpardonable sin of going to live elsewhere with his wife and child. She never got over that defection, which she took as a personal failure, even going so far as to write a novel about him titled *Game Over*. The tipping point was definitely my entrance into the world, unexpected if not premature. But she never admitted defeat and kept on playing pinball. After missing one shot, she brought in two backups. Françoise and me.

2

Françoise didn't much like her old-fashioned first name, especially since it was chosen by an unknown mother who abandoned her, even if the woman had her reasons, which Françoise later discovered. As soon as she took up photography, she de-

cided to sign her work with a new identity: Anne Franski. A
cross between Boltanski and Anne Frank, of course. Always the
same obsession with the war, with death, and with imprisonment. She never told me why she chose that name. Aside from
the obvious allusion to our family history, I see another reason.
Her life also depends on an enclosed space, a protective mem-
brane, a carapace. Each week, every other day, she goes alone
to her "annex," a medical center where she disappears for hours
behind tubes and metal plates. A motor's hum accompanies her
rebirth. In the hour afterward, she can eat whatever she wants.
The rest of the time, she is slowly poisoning herself. She was
born with only one kidney, which stopped working when she
was in her twenties.

Her most disturbing photos are the ones she takes during
her long dialysis sessions. Four whole hours for her blood to
be pumped out of her dilated vein, blue and quivering, then
passed through one of the two needles in her arm into a nest
of tubes and valves, of sphincters, of filters, a whole plumbing
system that beats at her rhythm, hydrating, cleaning, getting
rid of waste, and replenishing missing vitamins. Anne captures
suffering bodies shrouded in sheets and hooked up, like her, to
machines. Hybrid creatures, half human, half robot. She never
photographs the faces and only exposes details. A head of hair
poking from behind a sheet, swollen fists hanging in the empty
air, limbs surrounded from all sides by big white machines from
another age, as if they emerged from some futurist Jules Verne
novel. She also captures people who are lost, contemplating
the immensity of nature or the city, their contours always fluid,
dark shadows no one would notice, leaning on stone columns
with their hands held out, impossible to tell if they are asking
or offering. All her images reveal the human body's intimacy
and fragility.

3

Françoise Fondevilla, Anne Franski, Marie-Élise Ilari, Myriam Guérin, Annie Lauran, Marie Nélet, Myriam Thélen, Étienne Boltanski, Jeanine Giraud . . . this family is nothing but a long list of pseudonyms, of monikers, of aliases both purchased or imaginary. Names that are neat and tidy in order to hide others that beg the same question: "who are we?"

4

Hélène Macagon—if it wasn't Niania or Enta or even Entele Fainstein—also lived in the apartment until her death sometime in the late fifties. She couldn't have tolerated being far from Étienne, her boy, her "little king," the promise of a radiant future. They were never apart. Except twice. In wartime.

For the first six years of his marriage, Étienne put his wife in the same cramped apartment he shared with his mother, at number 84 rue de Grenelle, just above the horticultural society. Once he was promoted to chief of staff in the Paris hospitals, he learned that an old mansion, an *hôtel particulier*, a little farther up the street was for rent. At least the central part of the house and the two upper floors of the left wing. In 1935, the couple moved there with Jean-Élie, who had just been born, and of course with Niania. She took the second-floor apartment, which, thanks to its separate entrance, allowed her to enjoy a certain autonomy while staying connected to the rest of the house. She was there while still being next door. Every day, at around five, she would cross the landing and spend the evening with her son and daughter-in-law.

During the day, she worked as a physical therapist for young patients with spinal disorders. At her apartment, which had been converted into an examining room, she stretched them every which way, cried "straighten up!" and, once the session was over, instructed their parents to repeat this prescription. She claimed it was part of the treatment. She had no degree, not the flimsiest of diplomas. She never really mastered French—she could read it, but she didn't know how to write. Her medical career started in the trenches. Did she want to serve the country that had welcomed her or join her son on the front lines? Probably both. Like him, she entered the army in 1916 as part of a medical unit. She came out two years later with the rank of a nurse-major and a metal pin on her felt cape. Once she returned to civilian life, she became an assistant in the hospital ward at Laennec. Placed in charge of physical therapy in the infant surgery unit, she worked with a doctor, Marcel Lance, to invent a series of exercises to prevent scoliosis. Then she continued to practice this method in her home.

She never spoke much about her youth, as if that page had been irrevocably turned. Her past came back to her in waves, during certain seasons. In September, she would look all over Paris for corn on the cob, a staple that's now vacuum packed and sold in any supermarket, but back then it was almost impossible to find. As winter approached, she would preserve gallons of sauerkraut in the cellar. She only mentioned her own family in fragments, careful to erase the saddest details. She distilled them into magical, glorious tales. She would have liked to be seen as a princess, chased out by the Bolsheviks. Her father, as she often said, never carried a package in his life. She also used to say that before the revolution, one of her cousins owned oil wells outside of Baku. And then there was the sleigh, like a toy, pulled by four horses, sliding speedily over the snow to the sound of harness bells. In this Russian tale, most likely embellished, the only things missing were a winter palace, a dacha, a bailiff, and some peasants.

She claimed—and this was a lie—that she didn't know a single word of Yiddish. Étienne sometimes talked to her in Russian. He knew the rudiments of it, a music he'd heard as a child, which he hadn't tried to pass on to us. Some expressions survived him. The rudest ones: *nie marotch mne japou!* (get off my ass!), *sabaka* (jerk), or *ke tchortou* (go to hell).

I don't really know how Marie-Élise could bear to live with her mother-in-law. But I think she liked her well enough. She appreciated her whimsical side, her iron will, her incredible energy. Toward the end, Niania kept on receiving students, even though she could barely walk. She didn't know how old she was, or she feigned ignorance. When anyone asked her, she usually replied, "My dears, I can hardly be young anymore."

5

After Niania's death, the Bolts decided to visit Odessa. They took the car as usual. It was a long and difficult trip. After 1,600 miles and a series of mechanical problems, grand-papa announced he wasn't going any farther. He was less than an hour away from their destination. He stopped at a crossroads, turned east, and drove along the black sea to Rostov-on-Don, where the Renault 16 threw a rod because of some defective engine oil. He returned to the Soviet Union several times. He went everywhere—to Kiev, Minsk, Moscow, Leningrad. Even to Irkutsk and Vladivostok on the Trans-Siberian Railway. But he never went back to his ancestral city.

For a long time, I wondered why. When I was little, they said it was because he didn't want to expose his mother's flagrant lies by comparing them with reality. He'd stuck by her dreams of being a young princess, her wonderful memories of the "Little Paris" on the steppes. There was also, I think, another reason. He was afraid of what he might find in Odessa and also what he might not find. He feared, perhaps more than anything, that there would be no trace. A void. That was my experience.

6

When I have to explain where my name comes from, I don't say Russia or Ukraine but Odessa. And as soon as anyone asks me about my heritage, I say "Odessa." In my mind, that's enough. No need to add more. People who know will understand. As if belonging to that port city, fallen into disarray and mostly inhabited by ghosts, could take the place of both nationality and religion. And even occupation. Right away, the name "Odessa" gives off an artistic vibe. Given the jumble of identities I flounder in, this stopgap allows me to avoid embarrassing questions. Odessa, simple and in good taste. It's odd to claim a city where we hadn't dared to set foot. After my grandfather refused to go back there, it became a forbidden zone. A utopia. An imaginary place. Or maybe a vanishing point, that spot you look toward without seeing.

7

In July 2014, I broke the family rule. The reason? I was covering a massacre committed in Odessa two months earlier. The scene of the crime borders Vokzal station, where my great-grandmother took flight. The Trade Unions House stands in the middle of Kulikovo Field, a vast open space surrounded by conifers. Seeing it from afar, through the trees, you would think the Soviet Union still existed. A federation of republics built to last forever, massive, powerful as Greek temples. You have to get closer to the Doric columns to make out the soot blackening the edges of the windows. A metal gate forbids access, but you can see that everything inside has burned. It's nothing more than a big, empty carcass.

I was there with Sacha, my translator, the day after I arrived. That evening, two hundred pro-Russian activists occupied the colonnade, which had been turned into a sanctuary. Retirees for the most part. Old Soviets, babushkas in scarves who went to bed one night under the USSR and woke up the next morning in another country. And young people too, almost children, who wore orange ribbons with three black stripes around their wrists. In perfect silence, they listened to the harangues of a woman who was also of a certain age, wrapped in a tight, red getup. Loyal to the former president who had fled, people called her "Miss Barricade." She didn't give a speech so much as a stream of insults. She told them to "get off their asses," and go "crush" those Ukrainian "fascists." The words she used were harsh, violent. She basically exhorted them to kill their neighbors.

All these people had come together to commemorate one of the bloodiest days of the war in Ukraine. Their comrades died in the same square under circumstances that are still mysterious. Ukrainian nationalists peacefully marching in the city center. Shots fired. The first corpses. What seemed like provocation. And then revenge. The attack on the pro-Russians gathered in Kulikovo Field. The Trade Unions House transformed into a fortified retreat surrounded by a mob wild with anger. More gunshots. A fire broke out, probably from Molotov cocktails. Those under siege were caught in the trap, burned or suffocated. Others threw themselves out the windows. Bodies reduced to mush on the pavement. The survivors were beaten, some lynched. In total, forty-eight died and hundreds were wounded.

The demonstrators lit little candles that spelled out the words *nie zaboudiem* on the ground. Which means, in Russian, "We won't forget."

In truth, Odessa had already forgotten. It was summer. On Primorsky Boulevard, couples tangoed around the bust of Pushkin, almost brushing against him as if to pull him into their dance. A little farther up, an outdoor cinema projected an action movie. The screen, surrounded by columns and topped by a pediment, almost mirrored the Stalinist architecture of the Trade Unions House. Along Deribas, people crowded the café terraces. No soldiers, no police officers in sight. Only families gobbling up ice cream in front of pastel buildings coated with stucco. In the municipal garden, a brass band played some tune, while battles raged just a little way east. In my whole stay, I saw only one violent act. A purse snatching on Ekaterininskaya Street. The victim was a long-legged blond getting out of a black car with tinted windows. She didn't let it happen, clutching her crocodile bag with all her might. The aggressor ran away empty handed in front of an unconcerned crowd.

A white-bearded poet, Boris Khersonski, agreed to meet with me in a brasserie on Zhukovskogo Street, where he was a regular. He began by telling me that a local mafioso had bought the establishment during the nineties. In exchange, the previous owner got to keep a few hryvnias and his life. A practice that was apparently common in that era. I wanted to know how residents reacted to all of these events. "They simply went to sleep," he told me; "In the following days, the streets were nearly empty."

Like most of my sources, he believed in a conspiracy. Some move by Putin and his henchmen. The shooting, and then the occupation of Kulikovo Field, must be Big Russia's first acts in a reconquest of this strategic port on the Black Sea.

"That spark was supposed to provoke a general conflagration," he explained, "but the conspirators forgot one important Odessan character trait: their *beautiful indifference.*"

He said the last words in French, pronouncing each syllable: *belle in-dif-fér-ence.* Boris Khersonski loves his city, but he doesn't believe in its nonchalance, its alleged openness. In all the myths it boasts. "The worst pogroms in Russia were committed here." He lists a series of dates: 1821, 1859, 1871, 1881, 1900, 1905, 1919. Carnage nearly every ten years. "Odessa also proved to be very tolerant of Stalin's crimes," he added. Less out of fear, according to him, than through some form of detachment.

During the war, part of his family was exterminated by the Nazis and their Romanian reserves. The Jews, at least those who hadn't fled, numbered almost two hundred thousand and disappeared very early, during the fall of 1941. Birches were planted in Khvorostovskaya Square, where the deported left for Transnistria. One for each gentile who helped them escape. "There were only twenty-one," Boris Khersonski cried, "Twenty-one trees for a million residents! And among that handful of helpers, how many were informers, traitors, profiteers, snatchers of belongings?"

8

Niania must have had a memory of the riots of 1881, which followed the assassination of Emperor Alexander II. Several days of looting and murder perpetrated by vodka-soaked thugs with the help of the secret police. According to her passport, she would have just turned ten. But this was a fictional birth date. Like all the rest. She must have aged herself when she left, to be able to get out of czarist Russia all alone. Even at seven or eight, she would still have been old enough to understand what was happening. Was her house sacked? Did they beat up her father? Did she hide in obliviousness or did she talk to her family? In one of her novels, my grandmother describes Enta "crouched in the wardrobe, gasping, listening for cries, for possible pogroms." This formulation is strange. The pogroms are mentioned as a likelihood, not as something that happened. Like some nightmare that followed her into exile. I don't know if she ever ripped through the enchanted veil of her memories. She passed her fear of crowds on to her son and his descendants—her fear of that quick unleashing of collective violence.

In deciding to abandon her family and take the train across Europe, she also wanted to escape the menace that returned every Easter with the hail and the first spring shoots. From Paris, David sent love letters full of hope. It's an astonishing city, he wrote to her, where policemen see you walking without stopping you, without even insulting you. I see her walking down well-tended avenues bordered with acacia trees in flower where one year earlier she'd walked with her lover, his letter slipped in her pocket, bowing her head every time a uniform appeared. She must have had to lobby the *ouriadnik*, the village official, to get her fake passport, covered in stamps and inked Cyrillic letters. With an awkward gesture, she probably slipped him a baksheesh from her savings. Her two younger sisters, whom she had taken into confidence, were still called Kela and Rouklia, not Katia and Rita. They went with her to the station. Before getting on the train, she cried in their arms, then disappeared into a compartment with her black boater hat and her samovar.

9

First, I tried the central synagogue, which happened to be next door to my hotel on Yevreyskaya, the "Jewish street." There was a kiosk out front with a Byzantine roof advertising "falafel from Jerusalem." As I pushed open the door, a throng of children came out with tzitzits hanging over their pants. Under the Communists, the building was by turns a cabaret, a museum, and a gym before its resurrection in the late nineties, when a rabbi from Israel arrived. That morning, the Rabbi Shlomo Baksht wasn't there. His assistant sent me to the regional archives, which since 1921 have been housed in another place of worship a little farther down the same arterial street: the Brodsky Synagogue, which was once famous for its choristers and cantors. Had David ever sung there?

Today it's a Moorish-style building covered in a dark plaster that looks like tar. It leans on slanted wooden beams so it doesn't collapse. The facade is almost invisible under this protective coat. The hall of worship no longer exists, and the former nave shelters a bureaucratic beehive where dozens of tiny alveoli press together for five stories. The transformation of this epicenter of Jewish culture, which Isaac Babel mentions in his *Tales from Odessa*, into a storage center for administrative documents, mainly identity papers, bears witness to the ambivalence this city has for its history. Odessa behaves like a computer that never stops gathering data and at the same time never stops clearing its memory.

I found myself in a little cell with a lancet window, framed by fluorescent bulbs, opposite a tired, blond, blue-eyed man who was clutching a Bakelite telephone. Surrounded by old, dusty binders, his desk had an orthodox crucifix, a blotter, and a hand-cranked pencil sharpener, which must have dated from a time when it made sense to conserve office supplies. The employee asked me what my great-grandfather did. In a hesitant voice, I answered, "Opera singer."

"Ah, what a great pity," he said, showing the bureaucrat's satisfaction with finding an error on a form. "The Soviet Union didn't keep files on that profession." I didn't dare ask him why the Communist regime wanted to erase the memory of that group of professionals, especially in a city celebrated for its musicians. "And where did he live?" I didn't know much. People in my family said he belonged to a very religious household in the ghetto. But, in Odessa, there was no ghetto. Jews could live wherever they wanted. The poorest, which must have included him, lived in Moldavanka, a vast neighborhood that extended all the way to Pryvoz market in the north, also a setting for Babel's *Tales*.

"The Moldavanka neighborhood?" He seemed to notice my discomfort. "That's fine, but it's big," he said with an ironic smile. He wanted to know when my ancestor had emigrated. "No luck! He's three years too early. He left just before the census of 1897." I almost told him that I wasn't sure about the information I had. That David's birthdate, "May 4, 1854," seemed doubtful—forty-one years old, that's very late to start a new life. He could have lied about his age to avoid conscription, but I was afraid to raise that possibility in front of a representative of the government, afraid of jeopardizing both his case and mine. I was about to ask about Enta Fainstein/Hélène Macagon when I saw he was losing patience. He took off his rectangular glasses, wiped his tired eyes with the back of his hand, and concluded, "In any case, there's nothing I can do. The reading room is closed."

So I got in touch with Yulia, a librarian at the University

of Odessa. Brown-haired, with a slightly sorrowful air, she asked me to have tea with her in the municipal garden. The chairs on the terrace were padded, like at the Prater in Vienna. The sound of a fountain mixed with the murmuring of the patrons. I had contacted her through the father of a friend who had searched for one of his ancestors. She offered to help me. She'd already done it for others in exchange for a modest fee. She was interested in Jewish history and rounded out her monthly income by taking advantage of a recent interest in genealogy.

She wanted to be reassuring. Some trace must surely remain somewhere in the archives. She'd never run across Boltanski in the course of her research. "That name means nothing to me! But then, Boltyanski with a y is everywhere! As is Fainstein." She promised me that errors in the transcription of Cyrillic letters were common. The *t* could be a *che* or a *tshe*. The notorious dull sound, the mistake my grandfather suspected— was it hiding, not at the end, but in the middle of our family name?

Could David have been registered elsewhere? In Balta, for example, that city to the west of Ukraine that might have given him his name? "It's possible," Yulia went on. "In that case, we'd need to look at the regional archives from Khmelnytskyi." She seemed ready to consult all kinds of databases, to move mountains of papers, to comb through the administrative depths of czarist Russia. But she didn't put much faith in the story of my great-grandfather as the next Chaliapin. According to her, David couldn't have performed in the opera company because of his religion. The air of discouragement returned to her face: "You're sure he didn't sing in a little Jewish theater?"

10

I didn't know what I'd come looking for. Was it an address? A building? Biographical details? Tombs? The living or the dead? I walked around without a particular goal. At the entrance of the Moldavanka neighborhood, a blue trolley appeared, its axles rattling. Bearded faces drawn with a stencil stood out on a dilapidated wall, portraits of supposedly heroic figures from long ago in the history of the world. I walked down wide, deserted avenues. Here and there, the squat houses looked abandoned. Balconies devoured by vines. Grass and sunflower stems in the middle of the sidewalk, as if the vegetation had returned after some cataclysm. Everywhere, stoops gave way to dead-end streets, tiny courtyards planted with hazelnut trees, gardens surrounded by peeling wooden fences. Silence. There was no sound except the noise of small dry leaves blown over the asphalt, like a soft static of cicadas. No cars, apart from an ageless Jigouli that an old man was trying to start by pushing it along the pavement. Very few passersby, or none at all. A shirtless guy with a can of beer in each hand. Two other men in shorts with alcohol on their breath. I shivered as I passed them. In my great-grandparents' time, that smell signaled the presence of an enemy.

Retracing my steps, I was drawn toward a deafening racket. In a slatted garage, men washed cars, half undressed, tattooed to the bone, dancing to Ukrainian rap around a brand-new Land Cruiser. They punched the empty air with their metalworking tools, gyrated with their fire extinguishers, jumped in the middle of soapy puddles. Their water hoses created a halo of frothy light, kaleidoscopic against the rusting bodies of cars.

A militiaman in a green army jacket was stationed on the other side of the street in front of an official building. He watched this techno opera while cracking sunflower seeds between his teeth.

My quest was short lived. I threw myself at the smallest things that might trigger one of the memory fragments that had come down to me. At the Pryvoz market, I was overjoyed to see the stalls selling eels, the smoked mackerel and herring. In the evening, sitting in the little tavern that had become my cafeteria, I dove into plates of varenikes, comparing them with mère-grand's. I tried to put images, sounds, smells behind the shreds of history.

The first day, I went all the way to the Giant Staircase. Arriving at the summit, I was disappointed. I didn't know that, from the top, at Richelieu's statue, you don't see the one hundred and ninety-two steps but the six landings that stretch out like a tin-colored sea. The enormousness of the undertaking is only visible from below, from the harbor station, a pile of concrete that swallows the horizon. I didn't learn the trick until several days later, while I visited the port. Then I understood why Eisenstein chose this exact spot to film the squashing of the 1905 revolution. The staircase represents power, or the illusion of it. To the little folks gathered at the bottom, the steps seem almost impossible to climb. Those who find themselves at the top—the haves, the wealthy—think they're looking at a smooth surface. Hierarchy for the people. Horizontality, equality for the elite. For a long time after seeing *Battleship Potemkin* as a child, I imagined that the baby going down the slope in his carriage was my grandfather, a completely wild idea, since he was born twenty-nine years earlier, and in the Batignolles, no less.

11

The organizers of the massacre in Kulikovo Field were nowhere to be found. Every time someone told me a name, they also made it clear that the person was on the run, hiding out somewhere, usually in Moscow, or disappeared. Probably dead, murdered. No trace of the author of those first shots fired in the center of town, a local gangster nicknamed Sailor, or the assistant chief of police, a certain Fuchedzhi, who was one of his suspected accomplices. Nor was it possible to meet with the pro-Ukrainian hooligans from Chernoye Morets, the soccer club, who laid siege to the Trade Unions House. Odessa was like a giant washing machine. A huge crime scene where everybody tries to cover their tracks and erase, bit by bit, their slightest traces.

The day before I left, I got the number of someone named Alexander. Over the phone, he told me to meet him in front of the opera house. That he picked this particular spot, even out of convenience, made me smile. I watched him approach, a big guy, over six feet, used to taking hits and to doling them out. As the foreman at a cannery, he never went anywhere without his helmet and baseball bat. Just in case, he said. "As soon as I get a text, I hurry over there with my equipment."

On May 2, 2014, he was part of the attack against the pro-Russians. He would only call them by the name *kolorades*, potato bugs, because of their orange ribbons striped with black, the colors of the Order of Saint George that they all wore around their wrists. At the start of the fighting, he tossed several flaming bottles at their barricade under the columns. "That building, which Stalin put up, it's solid," he said. "But the oak door ended up catching fire." He confirmed that he'd helped those under siege escape the blaze by jumping out into a tarp. He swore he'd taken the seriously injured to ambulances. "But the healthy ones, we got them on their knees and we beat them up. That's only natural. We were mad."

12

There's one last explanation for grand-papa's refusal to see Odessa: the fear of not feeling at home in the very place where his parents were born and raised. Feeling like a stranger there. Discovering that he wasn't different from others but from his own people. Understanding the full measure of what they hadn't passed down to him. Everything they'd succeeded in forgetting, hidden in the deepest parts of themselves. The piles of twisted bread behind the glass in the bakeries. The smell of garlic in the halls. The squeaking of the trolley. The shouts of the newspaper seller. The hush that slowly descends on Friday afternoons. All the little things that make up their daily habits. And the vertigo of being alive, thanks only to exile and chance. Because of being, understandably, from elsewhere. To know that those who stayed were murdered. In *Ellis Island*, Georges Perec wrote that he could have been "Australian, Argentinian, English, or Swedish, but in the practically unlimited array of possibilities, one thing was explicitly forbidden: I could not be born in my ancestors' country, in Lubartów or Warsaw, or grow up there within a tradition, a language, a community."

13

A well-known Klezmer band appeared, as usual, in the evening at the Gambrinus restaurant. Its repertoire was classic.

After their interpretation of "By the Black Sea," Odessa's most famous song, the singer did "Tefillin" in Russian and Yiddish. He finished his set with a Communist hymn after informing a sparse public, in a joking tone, that this burdensome past was all he had left. Then he argued with the musicians about how to divide the tips.

Odessa is a Jewish town without Jews. Or at least, without Jews from here. Besides a few survivors. Of that past, only an attitude remains, a spirit, a little like the way people talk about ghosts. Specters haunting a castle. Most of all, humor, which has become their trademark, with their annual festival and their funny stories repeated over and over. A laugh, but from beyond the grave.

Anna Missuk was waiting for me in front of the Literature Museum, where she worked as a curator. It was nice out. She suggested we go into the adjoining garden full of buffoonish statues from novels about Odessa. "For Odessites, joking is like breathing," she said in front of one statue at the entrance to the square. It represented one "Rabinovitch" (here the Jew in the joke is always called Rabinovitch) looking up toward heaven with his cap tipped back on his forehead. According to a little plaque, the Almighty is in the middle of telling him, "Stay put! There has to be at least *one* Rabinovitch in Odessa." Anna Missuk stayed. As a girl, she sometimes went to the one last active synagogue, relegated to the outskirts of town. Every year, as Passover approached, she brought flour there to make unleavened bread. Her father, a bureaucrat and a member of the Party, didn't dare to go himself. In the prayer hall, she recognized a few faithful. "Very old people who had nothing left to fear." Even if the community was in the middle of a rebirth, she spoke about that world as if it had vanished. She was worried. She scorned both "Russian imperialism" and "stupid Ukrainian

nationalism." Between those two evils, she preferred the latter.
"Putin will take us to the grave," she said. As I left, I handed her
my business card, as if to correct an omission. She looked at it
as she shook my hand, and said, without showing any particular curiosity, "One of my relatives is also named Boltyanski. He
lives in New York."

14

Back in France, I took steps to help Yulia with her research. Before going in to the hall of the National Archives in Pierrefitte-
sur-Seine, you have to leave your things in a locker in the
cloakroom. Like a pilgrim to Mecca, you strip off coat, bag, cell
phone—everything you have, everything you are, everything
that serves as communication between yourself and others.
Even pens are forbidden. As if it's required to show humility,
renunciation, asceticism before approaching the past. Cut off
from the world, laid bare, I opened the gray folder that contained my great-grandfather David Boltanski's naturalization
papers.

His request was dated November 22, 1906. It was a form
letter, written in longhand and addressed to the minister of
justice: "Monsieur Minister, I have the honor of asking you to
bestow French citizenship upon me." So he was then living at
12 bis rue Descombes, still in the 17th arrondissement. Once
again, he claimed to have been born May 4, 1854, in Odessa,
but instead of a birth certificate, he'd only provided a "nota-
rized declaration" given in front of witnesses and a justice of
the peace. His father's name, Moïse, was on the police file. A
questionnaire followed.

—Applicant's total salary? 350 francs

—Does the applicant have personal wealth? No

—For what reason does the applicant request naturalization? All his business is in France

—What are his politics? None

—Has he lost all hope of returning to his country? Yes

—Are the applicant's father and mother still living? No

—Does he have any brothers or sisters? No

Reading this testimony provokes a sense of emptiness. David Boltanski drifting in space. Nothing anchored him to his launchpad. Nothing touched the earth. No family besides the one he'd just created. An orphan. A newborn. Unless all this was a lie. His answers must have been designed to help get his case approved. At the police station, they liked immigrants who were free from all ties. It eased assimilation and reduced the risk of more family following.

I sent my meager discoveries to Yulia. I thought Moïse, the name of David's father, might be useful to her. She wrote back to me two weeks later. A brief e-mail written in English, our common language:

> Unfortunately I have no more information for you. I looked for Boltansky family in Odessa and Balta documents, but found nothing. Sincerely, Yulia.

15

I never knew Niania. But I have a vague memory of her sister Katia. At home, in her apartment behind Saint-Philippe-du-Roule. A child's-eye view, at the level of a low table, of heavy glasses embossed with a brass crown, set on a lace tablecloth, and above, a hearty woman, dressed in a ruffled blouse, in the middle of serving boiling-hot tea and asking, in a heavily accented howl, if the visibly terrorized guests would like a slice of lemon. Probably a dream or a reconstruction after the fact. Like the image of her husband, Gaston, whom I imagine as Noël Roquevert, a retired officer in Clouzot's movie *The Assassin Lives at 21*—a sickly old man, sitting by himself in his armchair, snoring between two coughing fits.

When Christian went to visit him as a child, his mother warned him, "Be careful, this is the uncle who doesn't know." Gaston knew nothing, or almost nothing. That his sister-in-law belonged to the French Communist Party. That his wife's name wasn't Katia but Kela. That she went to Orthodox churches without really knowing the ceremonies. That the guttural language she spoke with her sister wasn't Slavic but Germanic, full of Hebrew. That the food he ate didn't have much to do with Russia. They met in a field hospital, during the First World War. She was a nurse, a volunteer like Niania; he was a convalescent. Each of them stayed in character for the rest of their days. He never got over his wounds. Always sick. Unhappy. A failed painter who worked as an illustrator for Michelin guides. A reactionary and anti-Semitic Alsatian. Under the occupation, he finally sensed something. Afterward, he would say, with pursed lips, "My wife is a little bit Jewish."

Katia was the first to join her sister in the early 1900s. Rita emigrated long after. In Odessa, during the civil war, she lived through the White Terror, the pogroms, the blockades, the famine. Their father supposedly died of hunger in her arms. She managed to escape from Russia with an Englishman, a former race car driver who became a farm equipment salesman. They lived in a big house in Brighton that was plunged in constant shadow. Broke and half blind, she spent entire months at the Rue-de-Grenelle, especially toward the end of her life. She stayed with Niania, who took her to Bourbon-Lancy, a thermal spa in Burgundy. Rita claimed hotels were always dirty and insisted on bringing her own sheets and blankets. In public, she developed eccentric manners she confused with elegance. Once, coming back from her rest-cure, she slipped a coin to the trolley driver: "You ave drizen vell. Ere iz alf a cent!" There was also a strange visitor who came from Russia with an opera he had composed who pretended to be a distant cousin. He never put down his score, even at night. After two weeks, he announced, "I'm leaving for America. You'll soon hear about me." My grandfather never heard another word.

16

Niania always goes out in her nurse's cape. Above her yellow star, she pins her Croix de Guerre, with palm, as if those two symbols could cancel each other out. She thinks she'll be protected by the arithmetic of that sum. One positive and one negative yield a perfectly neutral value. As she walks, she has to recite under her breath the ceremonial words from the awarding of the decoration, as if it were a magical formula: "Bravely fulfilled her duty," "without fear of," "despite being under fire from the enemy," "particularly at the hospital . . ." She's got the wrong war. She still believes in the cult of Philippe Pétain, "the hero of Verdun," and prefers to castigate his entourage in spite of the anti-Jewish laws he edits and signs with his own hand so that he can make them even harsher. She adores soldiers. Especially the decorated ones. One of her closest friends, Gustave Mantion, is a chief of staff at the ministry of war. A bureaucrat and ex-officer who can read the politics behind the cold, official texts. He and his wife beg her to be more careful. They say they're ready to hide her at their place, 8 rue de l'Assomption, in the 16th arrondissement. She agrees but continues to walk about Paris with her talisman pinned to her chest. She stops living at the Rue-de-Grenelle. From then on, the second-floor apartment remains empty.

Bathroom

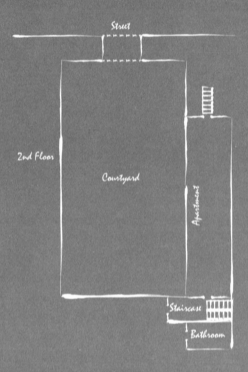

Street

2nd Floor

Courtyard

Apartment

Staircase

Bathroom

Perched on a stool, she looked in the mirror, making faces at herself. She tilted her head forward, turning this way and that, raised her eyes, scrunched her brows together, stretched her mouth tight, pulling her jaw forward, barred her teeth, puffed out her cheeks, and tucked her chin. She kept changing the perspective, so she could see herself from every angle. The mirror that hung over the washbasin reflected a fragmented image. Marie-Élise, Myriam, or Annie Lauran was multiplied by the four panes of silvered glass that formed the huge mirror. Each panel reflected a different part of her body, and each was embossed on the back with fine metallic leaves that were teased into curving undulations, feminine forms. Reflections from the glass separated her anatomy into pieces as if to better illuminate her interior dysfunction—her numb limbs, her atrophied muscles, her nerves that could no longer respond. The incandescent bulbs, lined up four by four around the white wooden frame, cast a harsh light on the mosaic of her face, making the bathroom feel like a performer's dressing room.

Even in this space, meant for preserving intimacy (implied by the lock on the door) she barely undressed. Sometimes you might see her upper arms, her hollowed throat, occasionally her bony shoulders or the tops of her little breasts above the neckline of her camisole. After a brief scrubbing with some damp cloths, she reglued her disparate parts by basting them with sticky products. She doused herself in powders, foundation, mousse, emulsions, regenerating cream, essential oils, spa water, hairspray, purifying masks. Bright pink lipstick, blue eyeshadow on her lids, blush, a swipe of eyeliner at the base of her lashes, self-tanning lotion on her hands. She used a different product for each piece of the puzzle before her. Instead of washing up, she got in costume, she readied herself like an actor before going on stage, pulling together the few visible parts of herself, creating a role and then sticking to it, like a crutch, so as not to fall.

To appear. Not other. Like everybody else. To refuse all distinguishing marks, anything that might be shocking. Blemishes, brandings, stigmatas, malformed limbs, clubfeet, limping, dwarf size. To remove even the slightest of marks. Paleness, chapped skin, sagging furrows at the edges of the lips and in the middle of the forehead, dilated pores, jowls, bags under the eyes, crow's feet, slumping eyelids, white hairs that stubbornly returned after each coloring. Sometime in the midsixties, after her first wrinkles appeared, she turned to plastic surgery. She had a facelift. Like some Hollywood star. She had her skin tightened, her muscles firmed, the roundness of her face restored, her neck smoothed. A perfectly kept secret. Private clinic, clandestine operation. Invisible scars passing beneath her earlobes and tucking into the folds behind her ears. A subject that was forbidden, even by allusion.

2

She didn't so much want to rediscover her youth (Rediscover what? The abandonment she'd been a victim of? Her godmother? Polio? The war?) or thwart old age. She wanted to escape time altogether. No beginning, no end. No path sewn with obstacles to avoid. She wanted to be ageless. A state that was neither tender nor ungrateful nor green nor ripe. Not canonical, but undetermined or absent. She would have liked to float in a vague space. Eternally in between. Clock stopped,

flight suspended, refrigeration chain never broken, a cryogen-
ically frozen or bionic body. She applied makeup for hours to
look like a porcelain doll. She lived in a perpetual present. She
didn't look back, much less ahead. She practiced forgetting and
avoided thinking about the future. The rare moments when
she was waiting for something—news, results, an arrival—she
predicted the worst.

At the Rue-de-Grenelle, we didn't celebrate any birthdays—
not hers or anyone else's. "That only makes the gift-giver happy,
delighted with himself and his good memory," she would say.
Good wishes and presents were forbidden. Everyone's date of
birth remained a mystery. Though she reigned over us, she
wouldn't be treated with ceremony. She couldn't stand the simple words "date of birth." Whenever she handed over her passport at a border, she turned so we couldn't read the numbers
on that shameful document. I can still see the officer, intrigued
by her suspicious movements, inspecting her papers in detail,
and me, seized with panic, afraid of being arrested for fraud.
On most forms, she left the space blank or else she lied. She
would slowly write out the day, the month, then change her
mind, erase the paper, turn a zero into a two and make herself twenty years younger. She preferred depriving herself of
payments to revealing her age, even if the benefits were large
ones like social security payments, senior citizen discounts, and
savings accounts.

By refusing everything that marked the passage of years,
my grandmother ended up extending this ban to all forms of
commemoration. She hated festivities imposed on a specific
date. Obligatory celebrations, everyone rejoicing on command,
kisses given at the blast of a whistle. As she got older, her dis-
gust with collective joy applied even to Christmas Day, which

she used to celebrate with splendor and generosity before I was born. As Christmas Eve approached, she shut her eyes and ears. She waited for it to pass. She hid from the television unspooling garlands, confetti, and false happiness. She avoided passing the lurid windows of big department stores and cursed the appearance, a little earlier each year, of sparkling snowflakes and white pines. At the moment France feasted, she barricaded herself at home or took refuge at the movies in the dark, empty theaters. Once, on December 24, Christian took her to a kosher restaurant.

3

She wasn't nostalgic for the past and distrusted her memories. Is that why so few photographs of her exist? Besides a photo that I found by accident between two uncut pages of *Game Over*, as if someone wanted to hide it. On the back, written in Bic pen, certainly not by her, there's a date: 1976.

She is seated. Dressed in a plaid shirt with big red checks, her sleeves rolled up. Her brown hair is cut to shoulder length. Due to an overbearing flash or the abuse of self-tanning lotion, her skin is orange. In front of the lens, she closes her eyes, refusing to pose, to apply herself to a rehearsal of death, to give the fixed look that resembles a corpse prepared for a wake, to show what was there and no longer exists, to put a good face on it, knowing that this face will remain when everything else has disappeared. But her resistance to the camera is softened by a lovely smile, a slight movement of her mouth that gives her a rebellious air and reveals her pleasure at being observed, at finding herself, once more, at the center of attention.

4

She was coquettish. She took great care with her appearance. In particular, her hair, which she dyed dark chestnut and wore in a sculpted undercut with a slight layering at the back of the neck. To avoid going out, she turned her palace of mirrors into a hair salon. As usual, she trusted the renovations to M. Bondu, a man who quite liked his liquor and used all kinds of sharp tools. He was later killed by a knife wound from his only son, delivered during a family dinner. He was the one who laid the blue tile and installed the mirror. A professional hairdresser came once a month, preferably on Saturday, to trim and color her hair.

Mère-grand would take her spot in a rocking chair, her head tipped back into a U-shaped basin, rinsing buckets of maroonish water into the bathtub. Afterward, her head would disappear into the dryer, a helmet full of hot air like the ones in salons back then. The noise of the fan, a smell of wet dog, nostrils and mouth barely visible as they went under the helmet, a femme-bot frozen there for hours. Once her hair was completely dry and her auburn tints restored, she submitted to a sharpened pair of scissors before applying a conditioning lacquer with a spray bottle. A product that made a fortune for one French cosmetics company.

5

For her, and for us by extension, getting ready wasn't a matter of cleanliness but disguise. Like at the court of Versailles, beauty products were essentially intended to mask body odors. She avoided the bathtub, that fracturer of hips, and she never undressed completely. She was never truly alone. A real scrubbing would have required nakedness in front of her children, which she balked at.

More generally, she was afraid of water. She found it dangerous. "Careful, it's icy!" "Careful, it's boiling hot!" "Careful, it's overflowing!" It could only be too cold or too hot, as if the faucet that mixed them didn't exist. In its cubic, stagnant form, water evoked horrors: drowning, scalding, flood, angina of the lungs, pulmonary infection, or basements full of Gestapo. In the morning, Jean-Élie brought me a cup of black coffee that he reheated on a little hot plate in the middle of the room. As soon as I had the wacky idea of washing up, he begged me not to drink anything before getting out of the water for fear of thermal shock. Nothing, not even the sugary brew that was getting cold in its saucer. My uncle still believed in the rumor that linked sudden hypothermia with the most basic digestive activity.

A polar cold persisted long after turning on the heat and didn't encourage long ablutions. The bathroom also didn't lend itself to intimate business. I couldn't flip leisurely through the lingerie pages of the Redoute catalog without someone immediately knocking at the door. It was a passageway, an airstream my grandmother used to reach her bedroom, swaying against the sink and holding on with her pincers. Our extreme closeness was paired with a great deal of modesty. We had to ignore these bodies that brushed against each other to avoid making a show of them. Despite its medical setting, the Rue-de-Grenelle's inhabitants hadn't been convinced of that important principle of public health—devoting a little time each day to personal hygiene. Christian never saw his parents take a bath and claims to have reached adulthood before he underwent his first thorough cleaning. "It was a shower," he says.

6

We were dirty. Me most of all. Black, half-chewed fingernails. A blue trail left by a Sheaffer fountain pen on the edge of my left hand, the one I write with. Long, greasy mane of curly hair, full of knots that my other grandmother (very particular about cleanliness, unlike her paternal counterpart) would attack with a detangling comb, a kind of pocket-size rake that tugged my scalp. The style back then only made things worse. Frayed bell-bottoms. Afghan coats still smelling like the animal. Green parka with a hood, trimmed with fake fur I liked to pull out in clumps. Clothes I wore day after day through a mixture of neglect and superstition. Especially my T-shirt, with large orange and white stripes, which I wore for luck. A pair of dilapidated, shit-kicker Clarks. Tati socks, which quickly gave off a smell of natural gas (one day my parents, thinking there was a leak, called an emergency number, and a whole battalion of firefighters showed up with their red truck, extendable ladder, water pumps, and axes).

The sixth-grade math teacher, who was a sharp man with the build of a waterbird, used some pretext to confiscate my book bag, an American army satchel from a surplus store behind Montparnasse Station that I covered with various scribbles. It had the inevitable peace sign, a circle traced with a clumsy hand, a line down the middle, and an upside-down V. With a disgusted look, he brandished his trophy in front of the class, turned it over, and shook it as he let it drop. It wasn't fastened. The sack and its contents spilled all over his desk. Sitting in my seat, under the contemptuous looks of my classmates, I watched it unfold: the demise of that khaki hump I carried all day, the disembowelment of a flappy growth that had become attached to me, and my own destruction. Along with this cast-off of the US army, some used Kleenexes floated in the midst of dog-eared textbooks, novels with ripped covers, lose work-sheets, balls of wadded up paper, dried and wrinkly clementine peels, pens with chewed ends rolling everywhere, and cookie crumbs. A spectacle that, with my clothes, got me the nickname Hobo for my first two years at the school.

7

As the former vice president of the International Union of School and University Health and Medicine, grand-papa had hypothesized this general principle: "In a clean world, we have to be dirty," he repeated, "Bacteria protect us." Not washing was, in his mind, a way of reinforcing our defenses. I'm sure he was thinking of one microorganism that had struck the household: polio.

At the start of the twentieth century, the first campaigns against the virus encouraged people to disinfect bathroom fix-tures and toilets, to make children wash their hands constantly, to maintain an immaculate cleanliness. In some American cities, during the epidemic of 1916, cleaning women of color were forbidden from entering white neighborhoods. Everyone assumed the vector of disease could only come from poverty, grime, contamination, overpopulation, the lack of sanitary fa-cilities. When, at age thirty-nine, Franklin Delano Roosevelt caught polio on an island near the Canadian frontier, the per-ception of the disease started to change. He wasn't a young child or a poor immigrant but a strong man from a wealthy family.

Doctors discovered that the rate of polio propagation was inversely proportional to that of infant mortality. The epidemics grew at the same rate as sanitary conditions, education, and quality of life. Polio was, in reality, a middle-class disease from a population obsessed with cleanliness. A particular scourge for those industrialized countries that were open to the world. The more parents protected their children from dirtiness, the less they developed their immune systems, exposing them to the virus when they entered school.

8

In the Désertines house, the "chateau" where I spent my vacations, there was no bathroom. There was of course a room on the first floor, glacial, with a breeze passing through it from a broken tile on the peeling wall. It must have filled that function a century earlier, because there was a white marble table with a porcelain pitcher and washbasin. A room left to dereliction, never connected to any plumbing, covered with dust and spider webs. To restore its original use would have required running pipes from the kitchen and, if possible, water heated to one hundred degrees or more to make up for the ambient cold. That would have meant a working wood stove or heater in the grand hearth and vents from one end of the old dwelling to the other—in short, a whole production, and a large household staff, which was lacking.

A hand pump at the edge of the vegetable garden let us extract icy water from a well. In the summer, when it was nice out, we put screens around the cast-iron tap and showered with a watering can, shrieking like birds, our feet splashing in the claggy mud. The sun was rare. Washing even rarer. To relieve ourselves, we had to go outside, usually in the rain and wind. A wooden hut on the other side of the terrace, opposite the stoop, was used as an outhouse. A terrifying place for a child, dark even in broad daylight, cramped, full of flies, and giving off a curious smell of feces mixed with scraps of compost and rotting plants. The seat consisted of a plank with a big black hole in the middle where ribbons of newspaper fluttered. Sometimes we found porno mags in the shack, abandoned by local youth.

Myriam hated her adoptive land, this countryside where she never stopped shivering, this enormous garden she couldn't walk in, this manor that would have made the perfect set for a horror movie. Désertines reminded her of her lonely school vacations, her life as an orphan and an heiress, the scorn she sensed behind the gestures of deference, the looks that told her that she wasn't from there and didn't deserve this house and even less the two hundred and fifty acres and eight farms that came with it. In revenge, she left the place in the state she received it. Since the death of her benefactress, she hadn't touched it, hadn't done any renovations. No heat, no bathrooms. Not even fresh wallpaper or a new arrangement of the furniture. It was as if the godmother had been walled in. We expected to find a mummy in her bedroom on the second floor, which had become a tomb. You could almost see the imprint her body had left on the musty bedspread with its mahogany frame. In the corner stood a spinning device, a wheel, where the whole house must have pricked their fingers before falling into an eternal sleep.

Water had its way with this plumbing-free structure. A hole in the roof that was never repaired. A slate ripped off where it was most exposed to the west wind. Constant leaks. Downpours several winters in a row. Beams under attack from tiny mushrooms. Wood becoming blackened and damp. Rotting that went through the rest of the building by capillary action. Blistering, collapsing plaster. Rusting iron work. Mortar between the bricks crumbling into dust. Slow fermentation of the rugs, the curtains, the great books with red covers, illustrated by Gustave Doré. The first cracks. The woodwork that disintegrated, followed by a part of the facade. The ultimate vengeance—my grandmother, in the last years of her life, left Désertines to decay. She didn't allow the prison of her childhood to survive her. A series of burglaries despoiled it of the few pieces of furniture that had been spared by water. Nothing was left. The house was sold for the value of the land.

9

At Rue-de-Grenelle, the floor of the bathroom also collapsed one afternoon in 1965. The space had rotted, but certainly not because of overuse. I suspect it was due to an undetected leak. Someone could have been killed. The tiles and the bathtub that rested on them crashed into the examining room. An avalanche of rubble fell on the metal table where a patient had been lying moments before. As if the house, too, wanted to be examined. A gaping hole opened in that enormous sick body and linked the two rooms whose functions were given over to it. Health and beauty in ruin. Clearing out, cementing, plastering, sealant, a rapid coat of paint—repairs done cheaply, probably by M. Bondu.

10

Unless you believe in reincarnation, human beings can't die and be reborn in another form the way places can. One day, the mansion on the rue de Grenelle will be bought in its entirety by a Russian oligarch, a Qatari prince, or a stock trader making a killing. At first, they will dismantle it completely—only the facade will be left. For months, helmeted workmen will come and go in the building that has been laid bare, lit here and there by the sparks of soldering irons. The carcass will echo with hammering and the whizzing of drills. Backhoes will make the foundations tremble as they dig up the ground. Cement mixers will drop thousands of pounds of mortar. And in time, the parlor will be home to a heated pool, filled with delicately salted water, oriented to face the rotunda. The other rooms, forming a series around the central courtyard, will regain their strolling function. Masterworks bought at Christie's will decorate the walls. A Rothko will hang in the old dining room, where my uncle's warring canvas hung. The cellar will be replaced by a two-level parking garage accessible by a slanted ramp dropping from the middle of the courtyard. Instead of cast-iron radiators, the heat will be diffused through the floor by anhydrite screeds downstairs, and above them large stone blocks from Jerusalem with gray or pink tints depending on the intensity of the light. On the second floor, they will prefer a dark brown teak parquet. A glass elevator will connect the stories.

11

So that they can install a Jacuzzi, the new owners will want to expand the bathroom, to gain spaciousness and light, as the realtors say. More literally, they'll knock down the walls, that unavoidable step in all interior renovation. But their project will come up against two obstacles. On the non-load-bearing side, they'll run into the stairwell, already reduced by the future elevator. And, in the back of the room, another stair. This one giant. More than a meter of difference between the height of this floor and the rest of the house. There's a simple explanation for it: the ceilings are higher in the middle part of the mansion, which was probably constructed at the end of the seventeenth century, than in its lateral wings, which are at least a hundred years older. So what? The architect will study the plans one more time and discover something curious—a fake floor, a pocket, underneath an intermediate space between the toilet stall and what was once my grandparents' bedroom.

In-Between

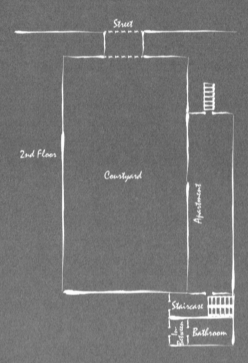

Street

2nd Floor

Courtyard

Apartment

Staircase

Bathroom

1

In the guise of a private study, he had a dark cranny, deprived of natural light, barely illuminated by a little bedside lamp. Stuffed with papers, clothes, notebooks. A cubbyhole, a storage room, caught between the bathroom and the bedroom, where he was only at ease during the earliest hours of the morning. A niche with two openings, which he used when everyone else was asleep. As narrow and airless as a train compartment. Just enough space for a table, a wardrobe, some wobbly shelves. No seats, no trappings. A double door that was always open. Barely a room. More like a pathway, a space in limbo like nowhere else in the house. Too small to be a vestibule, too large for a corridor, too big for a walk-in closet. It probably owed its existence to a fault in the construction or some kind of patchwork as the two parts of the building were joined. Was it a shrine? A chapel? A passage? There was no term for this architectural anomaly in building vocabulary. But the Rue-de-Grenelle's umbilicus had to have a name. Because of its placement and for lack of anything better, we called it the in-between.

Hard to find a hermitage less suited to retreat and solitude. He didn't complain. His territory must have been dark, cramped, and often violated by everyone walking through, but he loved it. It was perhaps the only place he truly felt at ease. I sometimes surprised him at dawn, standing in a bathrobe, deep in his shelter, rummaging, reading, murmuring, his lips babbling, his finger between two pages. He put his most precious possessions there, as if it were a cavern of wonders. His folders, in an old filing cabinet, organized by disease, in alphabetical order. *C* for cirrhosis. *G* for gastritis. *H* for hepatitis. *U* for ulcer. His suit jackets, hanging in the open air, some with ribbons or rosettes on them and others without. He drafted his lectures for the college of medicine in a clear, dainty hand on the back of old sheets already covered in black scribbles so as not to waste papers from last year's courses, sometimes crumpled up, thrown away carelessly, which he fished out of the trash. His collection of orange wrappers, the only obsession left over from his modest childhood—old, wrinkled labels printed with labyrinthine circles like Indian mandalas. And, of course, his religious paraphernalia. His secret altar. Icon, miraculous virgin, wooden crucifix, pious images with notes in his hand-writing, unreadable letters like tiny ant legs, missals, lives of the saints, manuals on piety, dog eared, bristling with bookmarks, endlessly reread and commented on, like we consult our elec-tronic devices today.

2

On the board of this Clue game, I've almost cracked his case. All that's left is the murder weapon. Hints are everywhere. Lots of fingerprints, witnesses agreeing, a profile that fits. In this in-terstice, he rediscovered himself, put himself back together. He entered in a thousand pieces and came out roughly mended but whole. He must have come to realize his own unity. The room served as his gateway between inside and outside, between his innermost self and reality, between his mother's imaginary sto-ries, his identity full of ruptures, errors, white spaces, and omis-sions, and the society he was trying to integrate himself into any way he could. He pitched between two worlds, between an empty past and an overloaded present. He was lost. He moved forward in life like a sleepwalker, in the middle of dreaming and waking. The in-between was much more than an interme-diate space on the way from his bedroom to the bathroom. It was his mode of being.

3

My grandfather converted. During his thirty-first year. In the prime of life. So it wasn't some youthful mistake or a Pascalian wager in the face of death. Still single, with the promise of a great career, in the golden twenties when France was carefree and festive. He wasn't moved by either self-interest or circumstances. No church wedding in sight, no particular threat. At least, not yet. A peaceful and prosperous world seemed to open up for him. Nothing demanded that he do such a thing. I can't imagine it was the work of supernatural influences—some bright light that might have hit him on the rocky path to Damascus, or an apparition on the top of a hill in Bosnia-Herzegovina. His heart wasn't sharply touched by grace behind a pillar in Notre-Dame. Neither did he discover something sprouting in him, like a little seed kept in darkness that waits for a beam of sun to germinate.

The step he took was voluntary, sincere, considered. As a nonbeliever, disconnected from all religious culture, I have trouble understanding that and even more trouble writing about it. I feel embarrassed to broach this subject, which quickly evokes, through a mixture of ignorance and fright, clouds of incense, prayers chanted in a monotonous voice like magic spells, twisted, prostrated bodies, mouths and hands glued to rosaries, crosses, a whole commotion, both mysterious and carnal, that is supposed to sway me and that provokes only my ridicule. There's also shame. Born a Jew, Étienne Boltanski became a Catholic. Abandoning his faith, and therefore his brethren, amounts to a betrayal. With an aggravating circumstance: he deserted on the eve of the worst, as if he had a premonition, to swell the ranks of the opposition, a church at war against his own, a church that always considered his kind to be the killers of God. Him, a coward? A renegade? An unjust criticism that ignores the context of the era and the traumas of a whole generation of pariahs, of immigrants fleeing persecution, leaving everything behind them including their shadows, to lose themselves in the country that welcomed them.

He didn't change religions—he adopted one. In this, he started from zero. For him, belonging to Judaism was holding on to an absence, a missing foreskin, the symbol of his people's alliance with the Almighty. He didn't worship anywhere. He probably never went into a synagogue, except on the eighth day after his birth, for his bris. He knew none of the laws of his ancestors, their traditions, their rituals. He was Jewish, aware of it after his mother's confession on the avenue de Villiers, designated as such by the anonymous posters, rude comments, and meaningful looks. He didn't hide it. He took it on without the slightest hesitation. He didn't take pride in it and he wasn't ashamed. Not once did he think of changing his name. But this identity that imposed itself was hollow to him. It didn't go back to anything. His parents had cut all ties that bound them to their original community.

4

I don't know what state his spirit was in when he traded skepticism for faith. Was his spiritual quest abrupt or gradual? Was there some physical impulse? Something missing? An emptiness that was impossible to fill? Something boiling up from inside him? I only know he suffered. According to Jean-Élie, his oldest son, "He was very much in pain." He fell into a deep depression. Maybe he even considered death.

Besides his rootlessness, the difficulty of placing himself, there was another, more recent sadness. A pain that climbed out of the trenches, out of that hideous butchering, where, in his capacity as a lifesaving doctor, he was forced to helplessly bear witness. Today, people talk about posttraumatic stress disorder. The psychological after effects for veterans are now familiar: extreme anxiety, turning inward, difficulty communicating, the feeling of being misunderstood by those around you, survivor's guilt, constant feelings of danger, the fear of being afraid.

He was still disgusted by his soldier's past. It taught him what humans are capable of. He had no faith in a civilization that was ready to use mustard gas and 420-millimeter shells against itself. Through its horrors and absurdity, the war had ruined the only belief his parents had passed on to him. He was still a patriot, but his blind love for France was gone. How could he trust a Republic that had just sent nearly 1.5 million of its children to the slaughterhouse? Even science had become suspect. His curiosity turned toward other avenues, such as the unconscious, dreams, the miraculous, the beyond. He could have followed his old classmates, André Breton and Théodore Fraenkel. He chose another church. Instead of a dictionary, it was the Bible he opened at random.

5

Before making a decision, he researched, tried things out, knocked on other doors. He questioned a rabbi at first, and disappointed by his responses, finding them too complicated, he decided to let his eye wander. Rather logically, he turned to the competition. It presented many advantages. For an agnostic like him, it seemed at first glance to be less demanding, more open. Most of all, it slaked his thirst for assimilation. By entering the Catholic faith, he once again chose France, the Church's eldest daughter.

It's not surprising either that he fell into Abbot Altermann's claws. In the twenties and thirties, that churchman was the universal converter. He transformed any currency into apostolic, Roman coin. He directed the Benedictine convent on the rue Monsieur in Paris, a refuge for many intellectuals who were hungering for the absolute, starting with Huysmans, two decades earlier. Grand-papa was easy prey. The priest explained to him that Christianity, far from opposing the religion of his ancestors, was actually the culmination of it, at once the most faithful and most developed form. He basically told him, "In becoming a Catholic, you'll be a perfect Israelite." A specious but classic argument, which he had thousands of opportunities to refine. As the child of Jewish immigrants from Russia, Jean-Pierre Altermann was especially interested in poaching from his ancestral lands.

His hunting trophies included the actress Suzanne Bing, the philosopher Gabriel Marcel, the essayist René Schwob, and plenty of others. This austere and sententious character was close to Jacques Maritain, who returned to the faith a few years earlier with his spouse Raïssa, another Odessite. In his letters to the Thomistic philosopher, he displayed the enthusiasm of a British master spy who has just managed to get a KGB defector into the West. "One of the souls which has received this divine grace, and I assure you I'm only the dazzled witness, has asked me to tell you of his happiness. It's Charles Du Bos," he wrote. "And you know what a prize his conversion seemed." François Mauriac, another one of his "disciples" who ended up escaping his grasp, said much later, "His converts are countless, but still, he counts them."

The ceremony Étienne readied himself for is generally considered a rebirth. It could also be a burial. On Christmas Eve, 1927, in the chapel on the rue Monsieur, he had to publicly abjure the religion of his ancestors. I imagine him standing up, before the mass of faithful, facing the priest in a white alb with a gold embroidered star, speaking the ritual words in his soft voice, the formula that was in use until the Second Vatican Council: "Having recognized that outside the true Church, there is no worship, I profess to be of the Catholic, apostolic, and Roman religion, and I renounce, in your hands, the errors of the Jews."

6

It would be wrong to see his act as merely a reflection of the self-hatred common in part of the Jewish intelligentsia back then. In his life, it wasn't a disavowal but instead another way to reconcile being Jewish and French. A way to impose a little bit of order on his interior chaos and even get back to his roots. Through scripture, he discovered Abraham's sacrifice, the exodus from Egypt, the judgment of Solomon, a whole universe he'd been deprived of.

He was also a pious man. As soon as his work was finished, he read the Bible or the most famous spiritual authors. Like Saint Francis de Sales, an early member of the Counter-Reformation. His *Introduction to the Devout Life*, with its echoes of common sense and its debonair tone, was what my grandfather used as a guide for his every moment. Like his medical journals, he examined it with a ballpoint pen and a sheet of paper for notes. He was just as serious, just as attentive, just as willing to learn. He spent whole days bent over his old spell books, weighing each word, looking for ancient secrets like a God-fearing man studying the Torah. In the bottom of his heart, he carried the same distrust of the world. He, too, lived a beggar's life. He had nothing, was attached to nothing. He lived in terror of doing the wrong thing, of committing a professional mistake, of hurting someone. Every answer he discovered led to new questions. His faith was wracked by doubt and full of fervor. His joyful exclamations were never without a serious foundation. He would have made an excellent Hasid—just among the just.

But this man was not very Catholic. I suspect he even invented his own personal cosmogony. Because he realized the uniqueness of his beliefs? His religious practices remained furtive. He practically hid them. I have no memory of him kneeling, his hands together, his head bowed. The prayers he said before dawn were confined to quiet hummings. He never spoke to a divinity directly. He preferred to contemplate it from within, like a mystic. It was a solitary pleasure. He rarely went to mass and almost never entered a confessional. More often than not, he stayed on the cathedral plaza, sealed in the Fiat with his crippled spouse. Did he prefer study to sermons? Or did he feel unworthy of entering the Lord's dwelling? Had this godless Jew become a churchless Catholic?

Despite all his efforts, he never managed to leave this in-between. He wanted to enter an eternal, Christian France. He was knocking at the door of a house that didn't want him.

7

In the eyes of the occupiers and of the Vichy government, his certificate of baptism had no value. "In terms of race, it doesn't change anything, just as a hundred baptisms can't make a Negro into an Aryan," wrote a doctor who was a member of the Institute for the Study of Jewish Questions, an agency created by the Gestapo for propaganda purposes. Little by little, the avalanche of decrees stripped him of everything he had become, leaving him nothing but a single three-letter word stuck to his chest. A frantic succession of German ordinances and French laws competed to more rigorously orchestrate his social death in preparation for his future disappearance.

Why did he go back to Paris? At the end of May 1940, with the German invasion underway, he was on leave in Désertines. At the bedside of Jean-Élie, who had just come down with early symptoms of tuberculosis, and near Luc, who had just been born. When the defeat was announced, he decided to take the wheel of Hotchkiss and get back to his unit as quickly as possible. He knew that if there were an evacuation, the Percy military hospital he was attached to would be pulled back to Royan. History doesn't say how he managed to drive through a country in complete disarray with a sick child, a newborn, and a handicapped wife. How did he cross the Loire in advance of the enemy troops, weaving between masses of refugees, and escaping bombs from the German Junkers? Of this frantic flight, Jean-Élie remembers only a night spent in a deserted chateau, abandoned by its owners, left at their disposal by a friendly housekeeper.

Captain Doctor Boltanski eventually finds his regiment at Ronce-les-Bains, a seaside town in Charente-Maritime. His superior, seeing him reappear out of nowhere, asks him where he's been and what he's doing there. He's suspicious, basically accusing him of spying: "how did you know we were here?" he says. The suspect defends himself, "but an officer told me . . ." He isn't welcome. All around him, people are talking about the "fifth column" of traitors from within. They already hold "Jews and foreigners" responsible for the defeat. He is put on leave without pay on June 18, 1940, four days before the armistice. What does he do then? He could have hurried to reach the future "free zone" in the south or tried to move abroad. He must sense that the atmosphere will soon become suffocating. Instead, he puts on his civilian clothes and goes back home. He calmly returns with his family to a city that has become the heart of the Nazi regime in France.

From then on, he submits to the demands of the new authorities. For each census, he goes to the police station on the rue Perronet or to the prefecture. He fills out forms that will soon be in the hands of arresting officers. He tries to fit his degrees and his ranks of military service into the tiny space provided on the official papers and understands, from their placement, that this information carries no weight against other responses: name, religion, racial background of parents and grandparents. He conscientiously fills out the list of assets, not forgetting the land in Mayenne inherited by his spouse. With the same care he gives his patients, he receives the interim administrator appointed by Vichy to take care of his fortune, clearly wears his label on the left sleeve of his coat, respects the curfew, obeys the ticket checker in the metro who tells him to get in the last car.

He does what everyone else is doing—he follows orders. Out of habit, out of loyalty. He continues to rely on the state. The law is the law. A good student to the end. His life conforming to a perpetual examination. To pass, it's enough to apply oneself, to respect orders, to eke out a maximum number of points on the written part and brilliantly ace the oral. He repeats that he has a good record. He believes that his medals, his titles, his career will protect him. The torrents of hate? The rising horror? Those are the fault of the Germans. His France, which he'd never stopped serving, wouldn't hand him over to the enemy.

What exactly did he know? He's aware, of course, of the names Drancy, Compiègne, Pithiviers, Beaune-la-Rolande. Everyone is talking about the camps. At least everyone who thinks they might one day end up there. Even if he doesn't know the specifics, he realizes that hundreds of people, wearing stars like his, leave each week on armored trains going east. He must have heard the English radio report the massacre of seven hundred thousand Jews in Germany and in the conquered territories of Poland and Russia. He understands that a machine has been set in motion, and though he feels its unstoppable nature, he minimizes the risk. He tries to persuade himself that other camps, work camps, this time, awaited those who have been deported: "It's not serious. They leave on the train and they come back," he says one day. Is he simply trying to comfort his family?

Slowly, his world crumbles. The space around him becomes smaller. As if he'd been caught in a black hole. Cafés, restaurants, tea rooms, the bois de Boulogne, bois de Vincennes, public gardens, theaters, cinemas, stadiums, pools, sports clubs, markets, concerts, businesses (except between three and four in the afternoon, exactly when most of them are closed), museums, libraries, exhibits . . . the places he's forbidden to enter multiply. He's not allowed to leave greater Paris, and he has to give notice of any change of address within forty-eight hours. First his car, then his quadricycle are confiscated. His group of friends, his so-called social fabric, also shrinks. Acquaintances, colleagues, former students, when they don't share his fate, they flee as if he were diseased. Some French people, seeing his cloth patch, offer their sympathy. Most of them seem largely indifferent.

In the heart of the war, he understands his Jewishness. It all comes back to him. How could he not side with the victims? He discovers his unknown brothers. He helps them as much as he can, treating them free of charge, offering medical care, responding to their calls for help, agreeing to write them fake referrals if it can save them, unlikely certificates that attribute what has become a mark of infamy to a medical procedure rather than a ritual act. He comforts them with words that rise up from childhood, words that come from far away. He is finally one of them.

When, on November 29, 1941, at the express demand of the Germans, the Vichy regime creates the General Union of French Israelites to organize the Jewish community, he decides to sign up. He wants to be part of it. Out of solidarity, and out of discipline too. All Jews were required to be members. One of his doctor friends encourages him: "You have to join. It will protect us!" He could perform a social service, make himself useful, while still following the rules, one more time. One time too many. This *Judenrat*, based on the model that already existed in the ghettos of Eastern Europe, is an ambush. Its directors and staff, despite the "legitimization" cards that theoretically exempt them from the roundups and internments, are all eventually deported. His spouse finally persuades him. "Don't do that," she begs, "That's madness!" She convinces him not to write his name on another list. Especially not that one. Her instinct is right. This organization, stamped with respectability, formed for the most reputable ends, and advertising its absolute legality, is nothing but a mousetrap.

8

She alone seems to understand how much danger he is in. Perhaps because of the people she grew up with. She's less afraid of the collaborators clamoring in Paris than of all those very upright people in the Vichy command. Bourgeois, for the most part, conservative and Catholic, followers of Charles Maurras, overflowing with resentment and ready to condone the worst. She'd been a witness to their "divine surprise" the day after the defeat, their happiness at finding they were among their own at last after being scorned for so long by the impious Republic. She knows what they're thinking and what they could be capable of. She is no stranger to their prejudices, their narrow-mindedness, their atavistic hatred for the "torturers of Christ." She knows them better because she's fraternized with them since childhood.

She has only to listen to her family. Her sweet mother expresses her distaste for "those people." "When you think of all the bad things they've done, you can't feel bad for them," she says in front of her own son-in-law. But he's different, of course. In those days, everyone has their "good Jew," the exception that proves the rule.

Or her brother, the same one who hangs around the Vichy antechambers and sings the praises of German order, the one who describes, in a joking tone, how much fun he had in the twenties pulling the beards of orthodox Jews—probably using a more pejorative term—when he was in Poland as part of the French military deployment to fight the Communists. His hatred didn't prevent him from having a cordial, even warm relationship with his brother-in-law, from enjoying his hospitality when he visited Paris, from swapping war stories. Soldiers always understand one another.

And the niece who married a viscount saying, at the Rue-de-Grenelle dinner table between two courses, "I saw a guy in the metro. He was looking at me. He had an ugly Jewish face. Oh, sorry Uncle!" There, I'm taking liberties with chronology. Her racist comments took place after the war. After the Holocaust. Before that, she wouldn't have bothered to excuse herself. All this was delivered very naturally, without trying to harm, without particular malice.

We can also go back in time. To Father Stéphen Coubé and

his lectures at the Madeleine on "the cursed race, chosen by God, ungrateful to God and rejected by Him," lectures taken from his book, which was buried in the office cabinet. One of the books the godmother had bequeathed. A curse she passed down. Was this author—a trumpeter of French anti-Semitism, incited by Édouard Drumont—also among the guests who came to admire the little orphan in her Sunday dress during five-o'clock tea?

She continues to frequent this group. She knows that those people might be moved by this or that case, and she won't hesitate to call on a few of them. But she feels their relief at the start of the great cleansing, their deep lack of empathy for all these pariahs as soon as they are considered as a group. She guesses at their desire not necessarily to eliminate this blurry mass that frightens them but to see it sent away, far from France. The growing menace frightens her more because it's familiar to her and echoes something she feels somewhere deep in herself. She's convinced: her husband has to disappear.

9

The deciding moment might seem trivial in light of the atrocities committed at the time. It concerns a cat. The stray had come in through a neighbor's place, through an open window on the other side of the courtyard, and pissed all over the place. The tenant in the apartment is furious. He threatens to report my grandfather to the police if he doesn't immediately get rid of the guilty party. Among other rules, starting May 15, 1942, Jews are no longer allowed to own pets. People in violation of a German ordinance, however minor, can be arrested.

The man has the upper hand. Though he has only a vague idea of what might happen afterward, he knows it would pose

serious problems if he files a complaint. The deal he gives my
grandfather is simple: it's him or the cat. He has no reason
to act this way. They've never had an argument before. They
know very little about one another. Before this, their interac-
tions were limited to polite words exchanged on the doorstep.
He's only a neighbor. But the order newly established in Europe
gives him tremendous power over one of his fellow men, practically the power of life or death, even if he doesn't think of it
that way, and very naturally, he takes advantage of it.

For the whole day, grand-papa tries to poison the animal
without success. He runs after him, grabs him by the tail; he
sticks various medicines between his fangs with trembling
hands. The cat escapes, wheezing and crying. He finds him
huddled under the furniture, his muzzle convulsed, his mouth
dripping sputum, terrified but alive. In the end, he managed
to kill him—I don't know how. He probably drowned him in
the bathtub.

10

He wants to flee. With the forged papers that turn him into
Miss Marple. But where? Switzerland expels most of its illegals
and doesn't open its doors unless it's an exceptional case: for
the old, pregnant women, children, and even then, not always.
No disguise could put him in one of those groups. He thinks
Spain would be better, a first step in getting to England or to
America. He talks about it with his wife. She's categorically opposed. In her condition, she could never manage such a voyage.
And there's no question of letting him go alone. I can still hear
her mocking voice, even today: "You, the man who never walks
anywhere? You think you can cross the Pyrenees in the snow in
a dress and heels? My poor fellow, you wouldn't even make it

that far!" She thinks he's incapable of dealing with the soldiery, the smugglers, and all the little businessmen who spring up along the line of demarcation. He'd be caught before he ever reached the free zone, those two lying words.

She dreams up another solution, which has two benefits—it requires no travel and it strengthens the familial cell. A cell that is more prisonlike than biological. She believes she's found the perfect spot to stash her husband. Steps from the conjugal bed. Inside, or better yet, underneath the in-between.

She wasn't the one who thought of the hole. It was one of her sisters' husbands. An architect from Pouliguen. Another veteran of 1914. I mention that detail since his gesture could have been motivated by the soldiers' bond that linked him to his brother-in-law. When he came to Paris, he often stopped by the Rue-de-Grenelle. I don't know who brought it up first, but I'll try to reconstruct the scene. He asks, perhaps, to use the bathroom, and once there, he's surprised by the few steps that lead to the in-between. The elevation of this narrow corridor in relation to the height of the landing intrigues him, even more so because it means there's a false ceiling on the ground floor. He taps the parquet and says something like "It's empty underneath!" He wants to get to the bottom of this—he lifts the slats and discovers the cavity is deep enough to create a hiding place.

To protect the secret, he offers to do the work himself. He comes back a few days or a few weeks later with sufficient materials. He takes up the boards. He reinforces the bottom part. Between two joists, he builds a wooden box. He includes a ventilation pipe, a barely visible grille where it lets out in the examination room. The shelter is about four feet high and three feet wide. A short man like my grandfather could kneel in it or curl up in the fetal position.

The trapdoor is padded on the inside, so it doesn't sound

hollow when you walk on it. In order to make it even more soundproof and to camouflage the hatch, a thick rug is laid over the top. The room above is dark and only used by close friends and family. But if the house were really searched, it wouldn't hold up for long. How to keep the police from looking for the fugitive in his own house? By convincing them that he's already fled.

11

Étienne and Marie-Élise decide to get divorced. Back then, the law only allowed husband and wife to separate by mutual consent. The conjugal tie couldn't be cut without a reason. I don't see them claiming adultery, and battery seems even less likely. In those two cases, a bailiff's observation is required. That leaves emotional abuse and dishonor. Did they insult each other in front of the judge? Knowing my grandmother, she could have found some pleasure in writing up fake letters full of fury. The creation of that phony correspondence, those spiteful pages, the litanies of recrimination, tears, groans, was probably her first literary experience. The marriage was dissolved by the 4th chamber of the civil court of the Seine on October 16, 1942.

His plan has to be relatively simple: wait for nightfall, pretend to have a fight, shout loudly enough for the neighbors to hear, leave in a huff with a big suitcase, and after a while, once everyone is asleep, come back on tiptoe and return to his den. No one had to know except, of course, his wife, the architect brother-in-law, and Jean-Élie, who, after his father's disappearance, would become the only mobile part of the family. Luc can't be told. He's too little. He might let something slip.

The sign to leave comes in the form of a green envelope inviting him to "present himself" to the authorities to "examine his situation." The letter, signed by the police commissioner, specifies that he needs to be "accompanied by a member of his family and to bring two forms of identification." He understands—or she understands for him—that he should not keep that appointment. That very night, he plunges into hiding.

12

The life he leads for a little over twenty months has often reminded me of one of my favorite books, *Rogue Male*, by Geoffrey Household, which was made into a movie called *Man Hunt* by Fritz Lang. The story of a white hunter who goes after a European dictator, a Hitler type, not to kill him but out of love for the sport, and who, after holding him at gunpoint on a Bavarian mountainside, finds himself hunted in turn and has to escape his pursuers by disappearing into the green English countryside. He ends up in the depths of a burrow, huddled in the dirt, exactly like the wild animals he was used to tracking.

I used to believe that my grandfather had also stayed like that, the whole time, hiding beneath his Persian rug, holding his breath until it was over. Since he didn't keep a journal and only talked about that time in his life through vague allusions, I could imagine anything. I see him in the fetal position, like a beast nestled into his den or a prisoner thrown in a dungeon with cannonballs chained to his feet, slowly taking the shape of his prison, and springing back, once the war was over, like a jack-in-the-box, all crumpled, twisted, hunched. Folded in half. Incapable of standing up straight for months. His pupils blinded by light, his skin pale and translucent from staying so long in the shadows, a little like a deep-sea fish or Gollum from *Lord of the Rings*.

13

Actually, he only hurries into his hole when danger approaches. When a visitor shows up. At the high-pitched ring of the doorbell. As soon as he hears the voice of a stranger. Like the concierge, who often stops by unannounced with her kids. He rediscovers his reflexes from the trenches. At each suspicious noise, he jumps into his shelter, hunkers down, head between his shoulders, listening hard for the explosion. As soon as he hears footsteps, he tries to identify their weight, their rhythm, their style—he follows them throughout the house with the same precision, the same anxiety he once gave to the trajectory of flying shrapnel.

The rest of the time, he hides in the in-between, his special reserve. Among his books and crucifixes. Always far from the windows. A shadow seen by a neighbor would be enough to give him away. At a distance from his youngest son too, the little one who thinks he's gone and feels abandoned.

In isolation from people, he retreats completely. He goes through a kind of spiritual crisis. Each morning, he chooses a passage from the Bible at random and interprets it to see what will happen. He immerses himself, as we've seen, in reading Saint Francis de Sales and other canonical authors like Theresa of Avila or Saint Augustin. In his oratory, he must also spend hours praying. He rarely looks at his medical treatises anymore. What for? They can't help him at all.

Nothing comes from outside but a muffled static sizzle. He listens to the BBC, the radio pressed to his ear, the volume practically at zero. He travels with the radio waves, trembles at each battle, silently shouts with joy at the slightest ally advance.

"Mussolini has resigned," he whispers one day to Jean-Élie, in English, his face radiant as if he'd heard a fabulous secret. July 25, 1943: Il Duce has just been dismissed by the king, and my grandfather doesn't know that he'll have to wait another year for his deliverance.

Twenty months. Without a walk, even behind bars. With only a few feet of cell to pace. No sky to look at through the grate. In solitary confinement. No visiting hours. Walled off in silence. No one to communicate with besides his spouse, his double, whom he returns to at night, once the two children are sound asleep. Limping woman versus man contained. Now they play with equal handicaps. Their conversations are limited to murmurs. Even lying in her arms, he is still attentive to the slightest sound. Getting out of bed, he worries he'll be surprised by his youngest son, in tears, the victim of endless nightmares. In the very early hours, he noiselessly leaves the room and goes back into hiding. He never really gets dressed, never takes off his old bathrobe.

His gray, empty days are all the same. When he doesn't speak to his God, when he tires of his books and the buttons of his wireless, what does he do? Like prisoners all over the world, he sleeps, vegetating halfway between waking and dreaming, losing track of time, not knowing what comes from dreams and what from reality. The space around him dilates. His microcosm becoming a cosmos. Even the war and the occupation seem unreal to him. He lives a slowed-down life, semicomatose. He hibernates. Once, Marie-Élise hears him snoring loudly just as a guest is arriving. She panics, raises her voice to cover his growls, and leads her visitor as far as possible from the source of the sound.

For the first time in his existence, he is outside the law.

Does he feel guilty? Is he ashamed of having become one more useless mouth they had to share their few remaining supplies with? His sheets of ration tickets are no longer valid. Without a few parcels sent by the farmers in Désertines, they would have died of hunger. He must above all blame himself for bringing great danger to those he loves. If he's discovered in his house, he exposes all its occupants to reprisals he knew would end in death.

Does he also think of Jean-Élie, only twelve years old, who is already taking care of everything in the house? He's the one who waits in line for hours to get an unlikely cabbage, a bit of boxed gruyère, rutabagas, inedible without lard to cook them. He also goes with his mother to the German military offices to try to get back their confiscated quadricycle. A crazy errand that only provokes the officer's fury: "Madame, it's your fault for marrying a Jew!"

14

The biggest risk? Being denounced. By anyone. The cat killer on the second floor. The owner of the apartment facing the street, a petty nobleman, a high-ranking bureaucrat at the Ministry of Agriculture and a great admirer of Pétain. The concierge, whom the police were always pumping for rumors. Her drunk of a husband, her blabbing children. The dressmaker from the 4th floor who swore by Radio Paris. The first potential enemies are the neighbors. His strategies are meant to deflect them. Like the mail he sends to himself from one of his sisters-in-law who is staying in Grenoble. Envelopes from the other side of France, addressed in his handwriting, provide evidence for the theory that he's fled from the building.

15

His experience is at once unique and common to most survivors. If not all. Everywhere in Europe, people hid in secret compartments, attics, cellars, farms, isolated houses, chicken coops, hollowed-out burrows in the depths of forests, under false ceilings or false identities. "If you didn't have an amazing story, you didn't survive," explained one woman to Daniel Mendelsohn, author of *The Lost*. She, like so many others, owed her life to a series of exceptional circumstances. Those who followed the usual order of things were murdered.

The most surprising thing about his case was that he spent the rest of his life in the spot where he hid. He was never far from his hideaway. When he entered the in-between, he was going back into his cocoon, this parenthesis that was never closed. Its presence comforted him. He liked to hear it crackling under his feet. He spoke of it with tenderness. He called it his home sweet home. His corner, his secret retreat. He would have gladly decorated it like a suburban house with geranium pots and garden gnomes. Before going on vacation, he put his few valuables there: his gold internist's medal, the silver, an antique Chinese statuette wrapped in a plastic bag.

The hiding place could come in handy at any moment. It was cleaned up shortly before my birth so that it might eventually house my father, who was a student and risked arrest as a militant organizer in a pro-FLN group for Algerian nationalists. As a little boy, I wasn't allowed to climb inside or even go near it when the trap door was open. It was indistinguishable from the parquet and heavy as a tombstone. When anyone lifted it, you could hear a hiss; you inhaled a cloud of dust and were swallowed by the pit. It was like breaking into an ancient sepulcher, giving off a scent of dampness and old wood. It was almost too dark to see the bottom. From time to time, I did open up this vault that both frightened and attracted me. But I didn't go inside. I never braved the forbidden, afraid of its ghosts and of a bad fall.

Bedroom

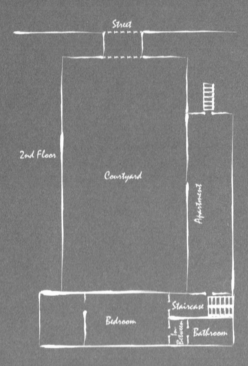

Street

2nd Floor

Courtyard

Apartment

Bedroom

Staircase

Bathroom

1

Since we used it as a trampoline, the orange ottoman was leaking along several of its seams. I helped it lose even more weight by bouncing on it with both feet. With each new impact, it whistled, spitting out a few white pellets, and its pear-shaped figure became a little more deflated. The polystyrene pebbles bounced around on the gray-blue carpet and disappeared under the furniture. Stretched out, her legs wrapped in a plaid blanket, mère-grand paid no attention to my antics. I could do anything—climb up on her raft of a bed, tap on the drum-shaped bedside table, wrapping my legs around the flared base, or I could bonk the white tissue paper lantern with the door so that it rebounded off the wall like a balloon—she would keep writing, imperturbable, on her leather lap desk.

Despite some hesitation, she even let me play with the blown-glass animals that were lined up on the counter next to the answering machine. She adored her Murano. She'd started to collect them after reading *The Glass Menagerie*. She took a wicked pleasure in imitating Laura Wingfield, that handicapped and nervous girl, shut in her zoo of crystal miniatures. Unlike Tennessee Williams's character, she was otherwise much sturdier than her translucent figurines. When I carelessly broke one, she remained stone-faced. She didn't say anything.

I'd never been so free and happy as I was in that house. I wish I could describe it with the precision of an entomologist detailing the life of an anthill, chamber after chamber. But if I did that, I would miss everything outside the lens of the magnifying glass: an incredible appetite for life, the moments of wildness, almost euphoria. Grand-papa dancing in his bathrobe, mère-grand sitting at the foot of the bed, crying out fiercely:

"One, two, woohoo!" as she threw down her last playing card. The tiniest pleasures. Anne listening to hits on repeat with her portable record player. Jean-Élie trying to split a coffee-flavored pastry into an odd number of pieces. Constant coming and going. The friends who showed up with no warning. The scorn for habitual rules of good behavior. The bare feet, the hands in the food. The possibility of saying almost anything. The endless debates. The energy, the exuberance that poured out of this commune that was hippieish before its time. Light in spite of the shadows.

2

The bedroom was decorated in the seventies style of the era. At the back, tucked into the corner, a big bed surrounded by plywood panels. At its feet, a low table with tubular, stainless-steel legs resting on a shag rug of long-haired sheepskin curls. Along the wall, opposite the window, a low cabinet was both a storage unit and a bench. In the middle, a big cathode-ray tube television was mounted on a rolling tripod. Behind it, Christian had built a wobbly bookcase held together at the corners with Chatterton adhesive tape and full of art books in thick cardboard casing. Everything was painted brilliant white, glossy, enameled, including the chairs. A color chosen for its brightness, its neutrality, its emptiness that broke up the dark colors and heavy ornaments of the other rooms.

This modernist bias was also evident in the paintings that hung on the walls. Contemporary work bought with Christian's advice. A red-and-white lithograph by Jean-Pierre Raynaud re-created an emergency exit sign. Transparent shadows covered in orangey Plexiglas by Lourdes Castro. A Le Gac showing two sky-blue silhouettes whose lips, reduced to a single stroke, flourished as though they were about to kiss, an intriguing view for people who barely touched. When we said "hello" to each other, we brushed foreheads, not cheeks. We tucked our chins and gently knocked our heads, a light and clumsy tap, somewhere between a blow and a caress, a little bit like horses nuzzling each other's manes. I have no idea where this ritual came from, and I've never seen it anywhere else—at least not this side of the Sahara.

Most of all I remember a painting by Breyten Breytenbach, the South African writer, which was mounted above the orange ottoman. It displayed him naked, in the "69" position with Yolande, his Vietnamese wife. She had his penis in her mouth, and he stuck out his tongue like a badly brought up child. A vividly colored canvas, painted at the Rue-de-Grenelle, where he stayed for a year and a half, long before he returned to his country and was arrested by the Boss, the apartheid secret service. This intrusion of eroticism into a largely asexual space was just as exciting as Vivien Leigh's opulent bust, which covered a sizeable area of the poster for *Gone with the Wind*, hanging to the left of the window. I was sure that this pair of breasts squeezed into a red taffeta dress was at least partially responsible for the burning of Atlanta that formed their backdrop.

3

At the end of the day, mère-grand ascended her royal bed of justice. An austere throne, covered in linen, king size. A firm mattress, thanks to a mixture of long and short fibers, and two goose-down pillows. Nothing else to prop her up. A bolster would have reminded her of Désertines. Even lying down, even in bed, with a rubber hot-water bottle always gurgling under her plaid blanket, she continued to exude an astonishing energy. She held court, received her close friends, answered her mail, typed her novels on her Olivetti, very fast, with two fingers, settled the accounts, took sides, made important decisions. The bed was less "the foreclosed space of desire" and more the seat of power, the steady center that kept everything together.

Jean-Élie entered the room carrying plates piled on a silver tray with twisted handles. Anne followed him, holding out a steaming meal in a casserole dish. We ate there, a fixed ritual. She would be stretched out; he would sit behind his little desk, right next to the in-between and his dark cocoon. We would kneel on the shag rug around the low table laden with food. We nibbled, taking some of this and that as we liked, not worrying about the order of courses. Our nocturnal picnics had the gaiety of a luncheon on the grass.

4

The TV was always on, but that never prevented us from talking. Quite the opposite. Our conversations mixed with the flickering television, turning into a hullabaloo without beginning or end.

The SCNF has returned to normal service this morning . . .

There's this really great Bradbury story . . .

The strike began with the dismissal of a cleaning woman . . .

It's always the person looking at the work who creates it . . .

Every father has a lump in his throat just thinking about what happened . . .

I'm against that house, it's no good [*sound of a lighter*] but I didn't want to go back there . . .

This will be the 291st episode . . .

It's the pits . . .

I feel, in reading your book, that you had . . .

I tried to repair it with glue and iron . . .

And under your relentless sun, Dallas, you fear only death . . .

The problem is the nation-state pairing . . .

J. R. you're such a jerk!

There's a very important concept . . .

I don't give a shit if you'd rather be with two chimpanzees or a goat!

But if we deconstruct reality . . .

It was impossible to watch the eight o'clock news in peace or
Dallas, Lay Your Cards Down, Apostrophes, or *Talking Back.*
We didn't quiet down until much later, during the Friday eve-
ning film club or the second movie on *The Last Show.*

5

I went to bed whenever I wanted, which is to say, when they
did. They didn't exile me to a separate room. I wasn't left to
the mercy of my childhood terrors, far from the brain stem of
the house. Back then, I had no space of my own. I stayed right
there. By their side. Behind the double door, bolted, when they
went to sleep, with an iron bar across it. The bathroom door
locked. On both sides, the drawbridges were raised in case of
attack. The dog, Nanouk, a filthy, cranky black poodle, stood
guard in front of the window, ready to howl.

Once we were locked in, the lantern off, four of us slept in
the same room. My grandparents in their bed. Jean-Élie and I

on the floor, in sleeping bags. Vessels that were still warm and humid from previous nights that we pulled out of a big white chest. Mummified at the foot of the family cradle. Campers in our own house, night after night. Tent put up, stakes planted, noise of zippers, of bodies rustling on the fleece, creaking parquet, in spite of the thick carpet. The same way Luc and Christian had once bivouacked in this space that was transformed into a castle stronghold. My father slept in his parents' room for fifteen years. His brother, for six more. Like a litter of puppies nestled around their mother for nourishment, forming a compact block. Only Anne slept apart.

Mère-grand's insomniac nights were filled with old American B movies, subtitled, with the sound muted so it didn't wake us. They flashed over her face intermittently, like the bright beam of a lighthouse in deep darkness. In this brief glow, I saw her look at us. She watched over the room from the height of her promontory, making sure no bundle was missing. In the dimness, her hearing became sharper. She listened to our breathing, recognizing us by our exhales, searching for irregular sounds, wheezes, suspicious coughs that might reveal congested lungs. Like an orchestra conductor, she made sure the sounds harmoniously mixed.

In her opinion, she had nothing to do with the delusional siege mentality that plagued the family. "My children sleep socially, all together," she claims in *Game Over*. "If I'm not there, they would lie still, their eyes wide open, with a sulky destructiveness, a calculated refusal." Or, a few pages earlier, "They formed a fat parcel at my feet, a little uneven, separate from me, with their own movements that maintained life, a warmth that wasn't for me." Or again, "The children loved me. We didn't leave each other for a second—they only drank life in as I filtered it."

At the end of our days, she controlled our nights. She kept watch at the door of our dreams. Like the Greeks, she feared sleep, the little, recurring death. Even that particular voyage couldn't be made alone. We formed a phalanx, a utopia without a strict doctrine, a socialist brotherhood in talkativeness only, a hippie encampment. A multiple body arranged in a star shape, for perfect conductivity.

In the morning, he woke us by gently shaking our feet through the covers. He started with the part of the body farthest from the heart to avoid shocks, he said, and to bring us slowly out of our slumber. With his wife, who usually ended up swallowing a sleeping pill, he accompanied the movement with a murmur, a song under his breath, a kind of slow melody. "Hello, Lili, hello, Lili," he repeated with infinite gentleness.

6

He's her prisoner too. In taking him away from the world, she saves him for herself. She has him under her limping feet, and in the night, she pulls him out of his cell, lifts her covers, and gives herself to him, becoming pregnant again. How can she justify the child she carries? Does she hide her widening stomach under loose dresses? Once more, her own body betrays her. Does she imagine hiding as well? She almost never leaves the house anymore. Bleeding, nausea, tiredness, discouragement, euphoria. The months of her pregnancy are wedded to those of the war. She waits for her deliverance.

She feels the first contractions as the bells of Sainte-Clotilde ring out, the carillons taken up by other churches, double notes pealing across the city followed by shouts of joy, cries that rise on the other side of the archway, the sounds of a crowd, a cavalcade in the street, in every street. On the other side of the

Seine, General Dietrich von Choltitz has just signed the order
to withdraw German forces from Greater Paris.

As soon as she understands what's happening, she calls her
youngest son and introduces him to a stranger. Did he remember the specter behind the curtains? The child recoils. She tells
him, "Don't be afraid, it's Papa, who's returned."

Her first act as a liberated woman? She exhumes the yellow stars from a drawer and burns all but one of them. As a
reminder. Then she crosses the courtyard, rings the doorbell
of the neighbor, the nobleman who works for the Ministry
of Agriculture, and forces him to hang a red flag out of his
street-side balcony, an insignia she cobbled together from a
rag and a wooden broom handle. A least this symbol exposes
its bearer to nothing more than surprised smirks from the
neighborhood.

7

There he is, outside for the first time. Just a short distance
to walk, up to a brass plaque. Another doctor opens the door
himself. Worried. The man refuses to follow him, afraid of a
sniper picking off passersby from the roof. Skirmishes continue
across the city. Étienne insists, "I'm telling you, she's about to
give birth!" He begs him, reminds him of his Hippocratic oath,
practically pushes him outside. The man might have said something like "Deliver it yourself! After all, we're colleagues." The
conversation becomes heated. After long speeches, the "colleague" allows himself to be convinced, gets his bag, goes as
fast as possible behind the crazed husband, hugging the walls,
looking up into the air, waiting for a shot. She's stretched out
in her bedroom; her water has already broken. The two men
get to work. The neighborhood doc is at ease. His assistant, the

chief of staff, is much less calm. She screams. And on her bed, her life raft, her throne, she gives birth to a boy.

8

The legend doesn't end there. A few days later, once things have calmed down, yesterday's outlaw presents himself at the town hall to register the newborn. The officer of the state asks to see the family papers, discovers the divorce, and doesn't understand any of the explanations. He's not happy about it either. He agrees to recognize the child's paternity but writes in the registry that the baby is "born from an unknown mother." And what first names would you like to give him? They had agreed on Christian, apparently inspired by the version of *Mutiny on the Bounty* directed by Frank Loyd. My grandmother was obsessed with Clark Gable, who played lieutenant Fletcher Christian, the leader of the mutineers. Hence the poster of *Gone with the Wind* just opposite her bed, which, besides Scarlett O'Hara's cleavage, also featured Rhett Butler in an equally low-cut shirt. So it was Christian. And also Liberté, added the father who had barely emerged from his cell. Christian-Liberté. But what about him? Was he free?

9

The survivors reappear quietly, on the corner of the boulevard Raspail and the rue du Sèvres. They get off the bus in their striped pajamas, the same buses that drove them, months or years earlier, in the opposite direction, from the Drancy camp to the cattle cars of the gare de Bobigny. They weave through the crowd, between hundreds of photos waved at arm's length, portraits that no longer resemble them anyway, with their sunken faces, their tranquilized expressions, and their hair cropped short. Once in the lobby of the Lutetia, a luxury hotel that had been converted into a repatriation center, they let themselves be seized by white coats, beige uniforms, ladies in hats. They are fed, powdered with DDT, and, in the cases where collaborators might have slipped among them, questioned, interrogated by police who make them jump and answer clumsily. Their courage is praised, as are their sacrifices, their acts of resistance, but nobody talks about them. They are handed a map and, if they can walk, a second-class metro ticket.

Among them, Zina floated in her clothes between life and death, with a swollen heart beating as fast as possible and her other organs atrophied. The newspapers published the list of repatriated people daily. Her name was on it. Myriam, her best friend from medical school, is there. She's been looking for her ever since she received the letter Zina wrote just after her arrest, a message that arrived months later, like a bottle thrown into the sea. How did she recognize her? By her Mona Lisa smile, which I still carry in my mind to this day? By her bright eyes? Her distinctive voice? The rest was gone. She hugged a packet of bones.

For a week, Zina told her the whole story. Her escape to Corrèze, her generous care in secret, the mayor, a doctor, who denounced her, the interrogation by the Gestapo in a school, her daughter entrusted just before to a dressmaker in the village, her letter, slipped into a classroom desk, and mailed much later by a stranger, the arrival at Auschwitz, the ramp with two lines, the one for immediate death and the other manned by the doctor strapped in his Hauptsturmführer uniform who saw her Red Cross armband and smacked her with a switch toward the left, the *revier*, the infirmary infested with fleas and rats, the chimneys spitting orange flames in broad daylight, the same doctor in a white silk coat and his experiments, liquids injected into eyes with the absurd hope they might become blue, sterilizations through X-rays, twins given blood transfusions from another type, vain attempts that played out in horrific agony, and the diagnoses, which she tried to cut short the day before selections, the lepers, the tubercular, the diabetics whom she tried to hide before they were captured by the same demiurge, and finally, her transfer in a *kommando* of young women, her forced march at the dull sound of the liberating artillery, three days, two nights in the snow, wounded feet in their clogs, the guards firing at their backs.

Everything, told for a week in firelight, in front of the children who pretend to sleep, in the icy great hall at Désertines. A house that was also associated with death. Irène Stora, the mother of another close friend of Myriam, was concealed there for months and stupidly killed just when the danger was almost over, in the chaotic days of the liberation. A misunderstanding. A soldier in the Wehrmacht who refused to surrender to the village militia, afraid he would be executed. As the daughter of a Bavarian antique dealer, she spoke German. She offered to help. Her calming words convinced the soldier to put down his gun. And then he wanted to take back his pouch. A gesture that was misinterpreted by the FFI, very nervous young men, freshly minted members of the resistance. Panic. Shooting. She was mowed down in the crossfire. Her body rests in the communal cemetery at the end of the garden.

10

Myriam also visited her niece in a psychiatric clinic near Nantes, where she spent years. Jeannette had been committed shortly after she was shoved into a carriage with other girls and dragged around La Baule by men who used cartridge belts for harnesses, booed at, called a whore, a bitch, a traitor, then shaved in public as part of a wild, pagan celebration, at once joyful and cruel. As a translator employed by the Kommandantur, she had fallen in love with a young officer. Guilty of "horizontal collaboration." The daughter of the architect who built the hideout and probably a few rows of German bunkers. She was shorn, verbally abused, covered in trash, exhibited in front of the whole, laughing town, dragged to the scaffold, to a pair of guillotine shears. On her knees before her executioner, her hair coming off in fat clumps, people jeering as they bared her skull. After that, she had the air of a hunted beast. Refusing food. She was frighteningly thin, and she stayed that way for the rest of her life.

11

The various spellings of Boltanski appear 177 times in the database of the Yad Vashem remembrance center in Israel. One hundred seventy-seven victims of the Holocaust, who were mostly from Ukraine but also from Russia and Romania, all with the same homophone, sometimes an *a* in place of an *o*, a *y* stuck in the second syllable or used as an ending. Men, women, children of all ages. Among them, 111 were murdered. The fate of sixty-six others has not been formally determined. If you count only residents or natives of Odessa, you get twenty-six hits. Reading the pages of oral history filled in by the families helps to reconstruct their life stories, their parental lineages, and the places and dates of their deaths. Almost all of them died inside the ghetto established in Odessa, probably during the 1941 massacres that were committed as reprisals for the October 22 attack on the Romanian general headquarters.

Joseph, or Yosef, Boltyansky's destiny was different. Born in Odessa in 1895, a year before my grandfather, he immigrated to

Germany. He lived in Mannheim, in the Bade-Wurtemberg, not far from the French border. In his papers, filed by his daughter, Khana Rand, in July 1973, there's a handwritten note: "Gurs—Rivesaltes—Drancy France." In the blank space just below she has specified "August 2, 1942. Auschwitz. Crematorium." You can fill in the rest. Hitler's arrival in power, the Nuremberg laws, the flight, while there was still time, probably to Paris, the war that caught up with him, the land of asylum becoming a trap. Interned by the French as a citizen of the Reich, an enemy alien after the hostilities broke out in 1939, expedited to Gurs, a camp in the lower Pyrenees, at the approach of German troops. Turned over two years later to the occupying authorities by the Vichy government, transferred to Drancy, then, very quickly, to Auschwitz, gassed as soon as he got off the train. Before he was exterminated, a Boltanski, maybe a distant relative, spent the last years of his life in France.

12

The chain had been broken a long time ago. He didn't try to discover the fate of those who had carried his name farther east. Pulled from his hiding place, he did what was expected. He returned to society. He started living again, like before, as if nothing had happened, with no complaints, without asking anything from anyone. He went back to work, to his colleagues. The chief of staff who had taken his place, the intern who rejoiced in seeing him wear the yellow star, the boss who was responsible for firing him. All those esteemed people who had hoped never to see him again. He didn't reproach them. It was enough for him to avoid them outside the hospital. Among his peers, he only spent time with pariahs.

He continued to accumulate posts and honors, sat on innumerable committees, but each of his activities required an enormous effort. Going out crushed him. He didn't walk. He couldn't stand the open space. In the street, he was seized with vertigo. He couldn't leave the house without a guide, as if he had lost all his senses. He feared emptiness, openings, windows, beckoning doors, stairwells. He preferred enclosed spaces.

He missed his hiding place, the crucible of his suffering. He'd never left it. Wherever he was, he reconstructed his prison around him. Only by building high walls could he find himself between them.

He wasn't a misanthrope, and had no desire to scorn the human race. Hate wasn't in his nature. He could even show compassion for his enemies. Jean-Élie remembers seeing him get angry at a man who rejoiced in front of a photo of German prisoners in rags, stretched across the front page of a newspaper. "A Fine Skewer of Rats," proclaimed the headline. "It's shameful to write that!" he cried. "Those are also victims."

But he lived in constant fear. The outside world was a jungle, full of dangers. Where could he go? What could he do besides isolate himself from others? In each of his fellow men he saw an assassin's power. Two world wars had convinced him: anybody could become a killer overnight if the circumstances permitted it, and it was even more predictable if the situation encouraged such acts. As the social psychologists said, everything depended on the frame of reference. He was half crazy. Or maybe halfway sane.

13

They got married a second time on July 12, 1945. No party. A simple administrative formality taken care of approximately one year after his extraction. Before posting the marriage banns, he wanted to be certain of the German defeat. She was in no hurry. She repeated in a tone that was half-joking, half-serious that she hesitated to normalize her situation. Her life as a concubine to her ex-husband suited her. The occupation and her coping mechanisms had accelerated a break with her class. She was no longer bound to bourgeois norms because the war had proven their utter hypocrisy.

She came out of the ordeal more fearful and more reckless. Basically, more independent. Without ever having been part of a resistance movement, she'd fought in her own way. She'd stood up to police officers, saved her husband's life, given Stora a refuge in Désertines, and at the concierge's request, she'd hidden, in a maid's room on the fourth floor, a young man resisting his compulsory work service in Germany.

14

Under the occupation, to cheer herself up and to escape boredom, she'd started to write. Once peace returned, she picked up her scattered pages and began to compose skits. Stories of mischievous kids, with her character at the center, playing queen bee. A faithful self-portrait. You recognize her in them. At once a little girl, a liar, loving, possessive, a hard-driving mother, a rebel chief, a professional agitator. Poetic texts full of love and revolt. She had her friend Adolphe Nuchi read them. He edited *Osmose*, which published them in one of its booklets crisscrossed with pastel color patterns that looked like ideograms. He encouraged her to continue.

The Woman I Once Was came out from Plon in 1955 with a preface by Georges Duhamel. Her first novel told the story of her bout with polio, the body no longer her own, invaded by icy chills, her first death. She also described her other war, the one that had just ended, including a lover whom she called Michel Barsky, not hiding under the floorboards but in the bathroom. And she returned to life, master of her own destiny for the first time, a heroine as well as a victim. In its wake, she put out three other equally autobiographical works, three outcries denouncing her adoption, the racism of her family, and my father's departure from the cocoon she had created, an incomprehensible defeat that she saw as a betrayal.

In the sixties, she threw herself into writing "true stories" about the excluded, the forgotten, people like her. Handicapped youth left to fend for themselves, Spanish maids who invisibly witnessed their employers' intimate moments, survivors of the Holocaust who were condemned to silence before society's amnesia, immigrants from Senegal or from Algeria who left in pursuit of a mirage, their children born on French soil, the "children who are no longer from there, not quite from here." She recorded their speech, re-created it from fact, with no attempt at style, following a literature that proclaimed the death of the author. With these sonic kernels, torn from reality, she wove her interior tape, her own concise and musical voice.

After reading *In Cold Blood*, Truman Capote's investigation of two young killers from Kansas, she gave voice to Samia, a girl from the Maghreb eking out a living in Vierzon, beat up by her father, on the run, sentenced to eighteen years for the murder of a driver who picked her up, and nicknamed "the diabolical hitchhiker of the RN6" by the press. She wrote up this bloody escapade trying to understand Samia's premeditated crime as a childish game committed with another girl who was equally lost and two kitchen knives bought at a strip mall along the way. Before their first meeting at the Fresnes prison, my grandmother had to accept the wheelchair the guards offered her.

Samia waited, inert, in a chair that resembled her own. A few months earlier, she'd thrown herself out the infirmary window. Fractured spine. Crippled for life. They became friends.

Finally, she fought for the old, another neglected category in France, which hadn't yet nationalized the pension system. In her essay "The Scandalous Age," she asked them to describe the hospices, the rooms that slept forty, the nights filled with cries, their exile, their solitude after their partners died, the garrets without running water, the six flights of stairs they could no longer climb. She also researched how children saw them by circulating a questionnaire in Parisian schools. What do you think of old people? The answer: they're dirty, grumpy, angry, good-for-nothing, they're not with-it anymore, there would be more space in the world, it's better to put them somewhere, in homes, in villages reserved for them, or else push them into the grave, make their death easier. Brutal words collected from two extremes of life. She combined them with gallows humor.

"Advanced age" inspired her fiercest writing. It was her last battle. No question of resembling those women, "grotesque, nonwomen but monstrous copies, altered, mimicking what they had been." She revolted. "The streets are so full of people who are already gone, but I can't submit to my ruin." To give in to old age, she wrote, is to no longer live, to wait for the inevitable. She called them the "dead living," "dead to love, adventure, hope, plans, creativity, to everything that moves." She contributed to *Mathusalem*, the "magazine that's not afraid of the aged," a feminist, proelderly zine created by Dominique Le Vaguerèse as part of antipsychiatry and hara-kiri movements. The second issue, which came out in 1976, had a drawing by Copi on the cover: an old woman, sitting with her cane in front of a tombstone, which read, "Boy do I want to die!"

15

During the same period, he did nearly die, without my knowing. Of what? I'm not sure. Something in the blood or a heart attack. What happened was hushed up. I didn't learn about it until much later. Like age, sickness was unmentionable. But I must have noticed his difficulty in moving, his tiredness, his lack of appetite. But strangely, all I remember is the sudden intensity of Jean-Élie's regard for him. From then on, he never left his side. He matched his sleep to his father's, fed him, helped him, served as his chauffeur and the ghostwriter of his papers, his erudite scholarship on dyslexia or the connections between psychic and somatic.

He even helped him get to the National Academy of Medicine, his final civic duty. In this role, which was beneath him, my grandfather had to watch the obituary pages and travel to the countryside to pay his respects as soon as a member of his division appeared in the paper. Each Tuesday afternoon, he presented himself at the hall on the rue Bonaparte to attend the general meeting, leaning painfully on his eldest son to climb the honor stair just so he could hail a few immortals who were barely more with-it than he was. On his drive home, in the Fiat, his wife scolded him for never greeting the right people.

Shortly after, he was laid out on the bed, which was transformed into a hospice. Half naked, with his legs apart. With all of us gathered in their stark-white bedroom. Jean-Élie arranged the pillow, emptied his catheter, cared for his brown spot, which became more and more hollowed, an infected scab he'd developed during one of his stays in the ICU. He who was once so modest let himself be tended like a newborn. Terrible impropriety before the end. He no longer spoke. His weakened mouth trembled and nothing came out. He was already elsewhere. Prostrate at his side, she smoothed his eyebrows, wiped his face, inundated his astonished eyes with tears. She whispered nicknames, squeezing him to make sure he was still there. We looked nothing like a Greuze painting. We didn't crowd around his bed to help in the great tragedy of his dying. While he silently endured his last days, we had to act like nothing was happening.

He was taken twice to the hospital—that bleached world where he'd once reigned. The second time he left the Rue-de-Grenelle, he was unconscious. She begged to stay with him, explained that her presence was necessary, that he couldn't live without her. Alone, he'd let go. He'd slip away. "We've never been separated, never," she shouted. She wanted to avoid handing him over to the attendants dressed in white, to enclose him once more in her cell, to protect him again—she gripped his icy hand, fuming about those people who "boss death around," and their "very clean garbage dumps." My father insisted on sending for a priest. Christian wondered if saying a kaddish wouldn't be more appropriate.

Ariane and I were spared this final scene. As well as the burial. For our own good, they told us. To spare us. I'm not sure if there was a real funeral. In any case, no ballet organized around the grave, with cellophane flowers and final respects. I don't even know where he's buried. Maybe at Thiais, in one of those huge necropolises south of Paris. In those cemeteries, death is so anonymous that it would make more sense to call them mass graves.

Once he was gone, she saw us as intruders. How could we keep on gesticulating, laughing, existing while he was no longer? We were guilty of living. She screamed at us, "Go enjoy yourselves! Let me croak!" She refused to get up. She kept repeating that everything was done, talked about suicide, demanded our help, one last time, some medicine, a drug to cut her suffering short. Then she hid her tears and resumed her life as before, or pretended to. She went through the motions.

At night, she looked for him. In the bed where she'd given birth, she was still anchored to the side that had always been hers. To her left there was nothing but emptiness. To her right was his little black table, which everyone avoided like a marble stele, and, behind that, in the doorway of the in-between, she could just glimpse the edge of the trapdoor in the darkness. "I hope he's still hiding," she wrote in *Resucideception*, her last book. When she stopped keeping watch for his return, she had the hiding place destroyed. She claimed she didn't have the strength to climb the stairs anymore. In place of the hole, someone installed a dumbwaiter.

Attic

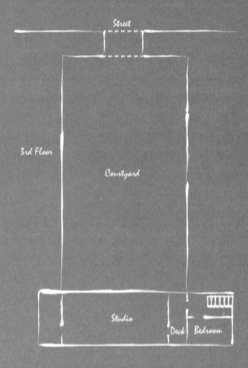

Street

3rd Floor

Courtyard

Studio

Deck Bedroom

1

I found Christian crouched, pipe in his mouth, in the middle of mixing clay in a plastic basin. He kneaded it until he got a paste that wasn't muddy or crumbly, then held it in his palm and sketched circular movements with his fingers, faster and faster, moving counterclockwise. His feverish, repetitive gestures, like a dervish in a trance, produced little marble-size balls of earth. He was entirely focused on his activity, as if he were returning to the origin of the world. He seemed to perform, or mimic, some long-held ritual of a vanished tribe.

He lined his results up before him, like little meteorites or sheep dung, in different sizes, sprinkled with traces of fingerprints and with rough spots, witness to a failure, to his inability to create a perfect sphere, as if he wanted to prove the helplessness of artworks in the "age of mechanical reproduction." He'd already made thousands, which he arranged behind vitrines and labeled as in an anthropological museum. His comings and goings were shadowed not by the litanies of a shaman but by the equally hypnotic voice of Jacques Chancel coming out of a transistor radio.

He stubbornly insisted on a material that was the enemy of form. As a rejection of durable practice and "real sculpture," he chose soft substances, spongy masses, like modeling paste, which hardened and then crumbled into dust. The Plasticine covering his paper airplanes turned into tatters. He proceeded with makeshift repairs, replastering holes, like an aeronautics engineer at the bedside of a Concorde that was shedding its titanium siding. He also made mysterious cuneiform characters that looked a little like Assyrian writing, starting from white sugar cubes, which, with the effects of humidity, disintegrated too. He fought losing battles. He often destroyed what he'd created and started over. He liked the idea of failure, the fragility of existence, the impossibility of saving what had been.

2

He lived horizontally, as close as he could to the plywood floor he used as a work table and a palette. Studios, with their easels and their big skylights, are turned toward the heavens, always full of light. Under the eaves, he looked instead at the floor. He could only stand up straight next to the columns supporting the roof or under one of the dormer windows. Everywhere else, he bent over, sitting on a low stool, a simple, three-legged seat for milking cows, or he stretched out on a ripped mattress of doubtful cleanliness that took up the lower part of the attic. Mostly, he stayed huddled, glued to his oil heater, prostrate like a frightened little animal in the middle of a chaos of greasy paper, detritus, half-eaten canned goods, tufts of frizzy hair, rolls of aluminum foil, old boxes, dirty saucers, newspaper clippings, clothes that still smelled like the flea market where he bought them, brushes with the bristles hardened from dried paint. His color-flecked pandemonium wasn't unlike the desolate spectacle of Francis Bacon's London studio.

He kept all his sharp tools there. His knives swaddled in white strips and his surgical instruments from the middle ages, hung from the ceiling on metal wires that sometimes snapped. His razor blades stuck on the ends of sticks, arranged in drawers by size in descending order. Even his corkboards were left on the ground, like some kind of bed for fakirs, with the balsa-wood backing always enveloped in hospital sheets. His forks, his pincushions, his halberds. Weapons scattered all over, which forced visitors to proceed with the greatest caution. He made it clear that he could just tug a pulley or release a counterweight, and one of his traps would spring. As a child, Anne impaled herself on a pin. The point pierced her calf. She still remembers a violent pain, followed by vertigo, almost like fainting.

The place was like a haunted-house ride, both terrifying and exciting. We didn't know whether it would become a hovel, a torture chamber, or an amusement park. It invited us to participate in a total experience that erased the barrier between art and life. Transformed into prey, the spectator became an element of the work. At the end of this obstacle course dotted with pitfalls, we found a wooden box big enough to hold five or six people. A panel half blocked the entrance. Once our eyes adjusted to the dimness inside the enclosure, we could make out a doll with monstrous proportions, dressed in linen fabric splotched with bloodred paint, wearing a laughing mask of France Gall. The creature had been on display for a few weeks in the window of a little apartment in the 14th arrondissement, on the rue Rémy-Dumoncel.

3

We had comical duels with a pocketknife, throwing it from the blade. Each time we succeeded in planting it in the floor, we would draw a rectangle the size of a hand around its axis. Each one tried to get closer to the other until our quadrilaterals filled the distance between us. The winner was the one who had conquered the most territory. A variation was to throw the knife close to your opponent, who then had to put his foot where the blade stuck. After several turns, you would find yourself nearly doing a split. The first person who gave up or lost their balance was the loser.

He didn't seem to draw a line between the moments when he

was playing and the more solitary hours when he worked. He fashioned many of the objects we included in our games. Cardboard boats, mountains of rough canvas and papier-mâché, buildings or gliders cut out of lightweight wood. He did make a distinction between his world and mine. As a kid who didn't like to share, he also whipped up playthings that he kept for himself. Marionettes, puppets, figurines. Characters set apart, with an ambiguous status—half toys, half fetishes. A whole bric-a-brac at once comic and worrisome. Like the enameled tin boxes pilled along the wall, which I never dared to open. Maybe out of fear that I would find something about us.

Ariane, Anne, and I were part of his installations. We had been absorbed by his wandering imagination. He had shut us up in metal drawers, behind bars, classified like the representatives of a forgotten tribe that would disappear if it was exposed to prying eyes. He used us like puzzle pieces to form a composite portrait of himself, which was also a portrait of the whole world. Anne loaned him her bunk bed for a pillow fight with bolsters; my sister gave him her wooden blocks; I lent my face, my hands, my gestures, my clothes. Striped T-shirt with short sleeves, thick socks, shorts, parka, sweater with button shoulder, basketball shoes. Odd how a simple outfit can trigger memory. When I found it exhibited in public, each article in its case on a sheet of cardboard, images immediately began to flow. I could see myself at school on the rue Hippolyte-Maindron, on the swings at the Luxembourg garden, perched on the wall of the alley, running in the garage of the neighboring building.

He concealed himself behind us. With other children, I stood for his youth. In one photo, I'm no longer myself but him at age ten. Wearing shorts and a shirt, which will in turn become museum pieces. The strangers display the same embarrassed air, caught standing opposite him, arms waving, like an

anthropometric display outlining the years that follow or pre-
date. He had us pose in the same spot, on the steps of the parc
Montsouris. The series ends with an image of him "at twenty,"
in an open shirt and bell-bottoms.

We were scattered among his rigged inventories, his imaginary autobiographies. Ariane when she was small, in her
bath, holding a flower or sitting on the flagstone in front of
the kitchen door, eating chocolate cream of wheat. Anne, or
rather, Françoise, wearing a headband, playing in the sand with
a shovel on Granville beach. The three brothers on vacation:
Jean-Élie, already grown up, his hand on his hip; my father,
wearing a sailor's cap; Christian, as a teenager, looking away.
The only photographs of our family that remain are in fake
scrapbooks. They're camouflaged by the same principle as Ed-
gar Alan Poe's purloined letter, hidden among other snapshots
taken of random families. Of supposedly normal people, Du-
ponts or maybe Durands.

4

By telling our story, putting it in a box, turning it into jokes,
petrifying it, manipulating it, mixing it with other tales, he said
he became unable to distinguish true and false. He had come to
doubt the anecdotes he recycled for years, that bedrock of our
family mythology—and so to doubt us too. These stories were
eventually nothing more than elements in an official biography
that was mostly artificial. Material for work that had to be impersonal, exploited in a quasi-sociological mode. Though we
started as subjects, we had become interchangeable objects,
mirrors returning each one's face. We who fluttered without
attachments, without consequences, we who, by virtue of our
fantastical origins, our particular customs, our refusal or our

incapacity to be part of any classified group, thought we were different from others. So we lived folded in on ourselves, and in the end, we resembled everyone.

5

The attic opened onto a little sloped deck where the dog did his business. A French window led to the main stairs and to a narrow room that Jean-Élie used as storage. After the war, tutors and various professors stayed for long periods of time in that room, isolated from the rest of the house. English, Irish, and briefly, a Frenchman, a Latin teacher named M. Laigle. Unlike the first two, who were staying in Paris to study the language, the third man was in hiding.

The presence of these numerous tutors added another singularity to the Rue-de-Grenelle: the children didn't go to school.

6

They take Jean-Élie out of high school during the war. As a precaution. For fear of roundups. And what secrets he could tell. He knows. He might let something slip. A careless comment during recess. A deceptive question from a teacher. The forked tongue. One word too many. He no longer leaves his mother. A priest from the Stanislas school comes to instruct him at home, along with M. Laigle—an old militant for workers' rights, a supporter of the Munich agreement who admires the new Europe. Between declensions, he likes to say, "We must not forget that the Nazi party is socialist above all." He's a demanding teacher who gives Jean-Élie a taste for humanities, languages, and great authors like Ovid and Tacitus.

A few days after Christian's birth, Laigle arrives at the Rue-de-Grenelle running, his face undone. He crumples in front of my grandmother: "The liberation committee at school is after my blood!" He claims to be misunderstood, professes his innocence, begs her to give him asylum—just a few days, until the storm blows over. She agrees. After all, the hideout is empty. Her spouse has just left it.

At first, they put him in the little room on the third floor. They treat him like a guest. They share their last food stores with him despite the hunger that dogs them. For lunch one day, they're gathered in the dining room around a can of sardines when they catch sight of a uniformed policeman in the courtyard. Without a word, both the master of the house and his guest dive under the table. The policeman knocks on the panel of the door. Jean-Élie goes to open it. The man complains of a stomach ache, asking to be examined: "They told me a doctor lives here."

After two weeks, M. Laigle thanks them and leaves. For years, they hear nothing of him.

7

In October 1944, after being absent for four years, Jean-Élie returned to Louis-le-Grand lycée. He passed his exams the year after.

Once peacetime returned, Luc followed an equally erratic curriculum. He missed class for several months of the year, sometimes a whole trimester (usually the second one, from December to February). When by some miracle he did show up for school, his teachers reproached him for being absentminded. They wondered if he hadn't developed some form of cretinism. Not until age fifteen did they detect his deafness.

Christian refused to go to school. He grabbed the lamp posts on the way and screamed as if they were taking him to the slaughterhouse. After a chaotic primary school education that was intermittently carried out at several nearby Catholic establishments where they called him "little rabbi," he was taken out of class for good around age ten.

Their mother claimed each of them had health problems and brandished doctor's notes from her husband declaring that they were all more or less incapable of school.

She was revolted by everything that reminded her of her own childhood, including the teaching profession. Memories of time-outs and whacks from rulers, or school teachers whom she confused with her godmother. She hated those people she called "certified tormentors," was horrified by curricula, rules, schedules. She scorned the state and its representatives. Above all, she was leery of an institution that competed with her authority over her sons, and even worse, took them from her side. The school term was her worst enemy.

She transformed herself into a schoolmistress. She shut her children up in her vault and taught them multiplication tables, pinching them when they made a mistake. Grammar book in hand, she went to war against their bad spelling. She had them recite long lists of exceptions like psalms on a rosary. In the end, she got a career out of it. She became a speech pathologist. She mostly worked with children who stuttered or had dyslexia. I was one of her most tireless students. Every Wednesday afternoon for years, I would sit next to her at grand-papa's little table, facing a blackboard on a stand. I would take a white piece of chalk from the easel's gutter and, under her dictation, trace with a hesitant hand the words I imagined as traps hurrying to catch me.

8

The three brothers lived in isolation. They didn't have friends. They hadn't spent enough time in the same school to make any, and they hesitated to bring a foreign body into their den.

Left to themselves, they created laws, a president, a parliament. Their republic was fragile. The youngest played the leader of the putsch. He incited coups d'état, invaded territories, reigned over the arrangement of tables and chairs. The other boy, a little older, represented the revolution. He put up barricades and created a state of permanent agitation. Their older brother was the judge. He was the high court, negotiating fleeting peace treaties, watching over the fair process of elections, dealing out justice with a firm hand during public trials. The toilet was the prison. A baby gate served as a guillotine, stretched like an accordion across a doorway.

Luc kept all kinds of beastlings. Rabbit, turtle, cat, dog. Especially pigeons. Not the dirty, gray ones from the street but their more noble cousins: diamond doves, peacock pigeons with spreading tails, turtledoves with gray heads and a red shimmer on their bodies. Couples, with the exception of one capuchin pigeon with an ermine collar, who, naturally, cooed all day, bobbing his head in an incessant back and forth. He transformed the deck into an aviary to give them some space to frolic, covering the only open-air part of the house with a metallic trellis. In their park behind bars, the birds lived with the other animals. Some drama ensued. The rabbit would chew on any feathers that came within range of his incisors. One day he lured a turtledove into his burrow and suffocated it. In winter, when it was very cold, Luc repatriated the animal farm to his room. The dresser where the seven birds stayed was whitened with droppings. It was hard to say which was worse, the smell or the screeches.

9

Despite his freedman's name, Christian-Liberté never left his family. He could spend hours doing nothing, never opening his mouth. To keep him busy, Jean-Élie brought him everywhere. The child went with him to the Sorbonne and sat quietly in the lecture hall, waiting for the end of class. At home, he watched TV with his grandmother, played with his toy soldiers on the floor, and made up stories. The hiding place obsessed him— that dirty, dark hole where he wasn't allowed to go. To him, it was proof that the Rue-de-Grenelle concealed either horrors or marvels. He dug into the walls, looking for treasures. In his cage, nothing was forbidden. He could do anything except go outside.

Did imprisonment encourage creativity? The imagination developing more easily because it wasn't confronted with reality? At thirteen, the youngest was already breathing life into some modeling clay golem when the middle brother told him, "that's a pretty thing you're making." He looked differently at the half-formed shape between his fingers and, from modeling, gravitated toward a more pictorial form of representation. He started to make bigger and bigger paintings on plywood boards. While he painted massacres of innocents or cities in flames, the eldest taught him history or English. He ended up acquiring the wisdom of a bard.

Totally by chance, he showed up for the baccalaureate exam on the first day of the orals. When they heard about it, his parents didn't hold out much hope that he would pass. The night before the results came out, they were surprised to hear M. Laigle's voice over the phone. They'd heard nothing from the Latin professor since the liberation. "Your son passed his exam," he told them, before hanging up. He was part of the jury. Maybe the head of it. Christian, who never took the written test, is convinced he owes his half diploma to the goodwill of a former collaborator.

Intrigued by his obsession with painting and unable to judge its value, his father sent him to see André Breton. His old classmate from Chaptal received the teenager at home, in his studio on the boulevard de Clichy, among his masks and fetishes. "You seem very nice," he said. "Don't become an artist. They're all wicked. It's a dirty field."

10

Luc was the first to break out of the magic circle around the redemptive bed. When he was about fifteen, he claimed the up-stairs bedroom. An extraordinary demand. Leaving the strong-hold where his family retreated every night amounted to a declaration of independence. Taking off in search of adventure. He exiled himself from the walls. He moved to a place where his mother never went, where she practically couldn't climb, at least not without undertaking a perilous journey, gripping an old rope held by metal rings that stood in for a bannister and wiggled the length of the stairs. Living in the attic was the same as having one foot out the door.

A headstrong, restless, tormented character, he hoped for a monastic and individual space. He started inviting friends over to his eagle's perch. The first time he hosted a girl, his mother stood at the bottom of the stairs and shouted in her low, mocking tone, the voice of a she wolf disguised as an old lady, "It smells like fresh meat!" Guaranteed result: it was a long time before he dared to bring home another person of the opposite sex.

He started to walk places alone. He went to cafés in the Latin Quarter, which seemed like the other side of the world. He abandoned his anchorite life for a group of friends. His own. Philippe, Guy, Alain, Jean-Jacques, Monique. He brought them together in a back room, around a small, hand-mimeographed pamphlet. A leaflet of poetry that he'd opportunely baptized: *Emergency Exit*. Each copy contained a card for subscriptions: ordinary (six hundred francs) or sponsor (one thousand). These could be sent to his address, rue de Grenelle, Paris, 7th.

From adolescence on, he spent his time reading and writing poems. Lines torn from his anxious childhood, with lullaby rhythms, about guns, mutilations, and a little Jewish orphan.

11

They burned my daddy
They gutted my maman
Her body rested over there
Near the hangman and his wheel
Near his blade made out of steel
Pressed in mud laced with tacks
The lungs, the wounds, and her cheeks

They made gold teeth from her wedding rings
So fat white girls
Can gobble sausage links

They mixed her blood with mulch
So that brave fools
Can drink their beer at the Munich festival

The orphan Jew has a painful face
The orphan Jew knows too many landscapes

The baker was one of the hangman's men
The bus driver led the jury
The park attendant held the torch
And the butcher laughed his fury
Before my torn maman

That smile, that smile
It was two minutes before the kill!

With her fat they made suet
They mixed her blood in with the mulch
They have forgotten the orphan Jew
And his hatred and his hatred

12

I stumbled on a mildewed issue of *Emergency Exit* as I was
cleaning out my mother's house after her death. The apartment,
which occupied the first floor of a Haussmann-style building on
the rue Philibert-Lucot, had already been turned upside down,
as if there had been a burglary. Rooms that smelled like the
grave. Empty things turned on their sides, looking for takers.
Clothes destined for the church bin stuffed quickly into garbage

bags. The pamphlet was in a mahogany bookcase whose contents had escaped the morning's raid by a bookseller. Besides the subscription card, two yellowed tracts were folded inside, preserved for half a century like love letters.

The first, titled "Soldier: Where Are Your Enemies?" called for rebellion among conscripts serving in Algeria.

In the name of your duty as a Frenchman and a free man:

- Refuse to participate in organized massacres, atrocities, torturing of Algerian resistance fighters.
- Respect prisoners and "suspects" under arrest and treat them as you would like to be treated! They have a right to life, to food and water, a right not to be beaten, tortured or killed.
- Resist the pressure from fascist elements of the army and push back against the killer's role they force you to perform. As long as you continue, the soldiers of the National Liberation Army will be forced to ambush you to liberate their country.
- Fight for your liberation and Algeria's!!!
- We support you!

The text comes from "a group of young French people" which included draft dodgers and deserters in their ranks. In the margin of the sheet, someone—was it my mother?—had written a sort of note low on the page that didn't have to do with anything except, perhaps, a later judgment on this episode of her youth: "the humility, the clumsiness, the bleak stubbornness . . ."

The second letter wasn't destined for the public. It ordered the "patient work of agitation and provocation" before they could create "a certain idea of madness and scandal" in French opinion. To arrive at this goal, its author recommended that they expand the circle of conspirators:

We must involve as many people as possible in our secret battle, especially those who can slip materials from hand to hand. They risk nothing, since they don't do anything else. Everyone should come up with a list of friends who are likely to be interested.

Printers, peddlers, people putting up posters all had to recognize their target places: "lecture halls, hostels, city universities, schools, movie theaters, cafeterias"; wait until 11 p.m. before posting sheets or drawing graffiti on the walls; avoid tagging things near your house; don't write anything out by hand, not even the addresses on the backs of envelopes. A perfect propagandist's guide.

> And above all, report to us periodically on how the details of these activities are going. Count the materials handed out so that each person can tell us the exactly where it's been deployed . . . Use pseudonyms in the report.
>
> Thanks and in brotherhood,
>
> Christophe

Who was Christophe? Surely an alias. Identical typed characters and paper quality, phrased and presented in the same way. Everything led me to think that the two letters came from the same source, which was written in bold on the internal bulletin: "FAM, French Anti-colonialist Movement. Dimitrov Unit."

13

They always maintained the mystery around their involvement, as if they'd never really got out of it and still feared some judicial consequences despite the amnesties that followed. "We

were in support" is all my father would say. He claimed that
his role was limited to distributing literature for the movement
following the modus operandi above. "Your mother was much
more active than I was," he repeated, without being more precise. They had met during a meeting of the Dimitrov Unit held
in a bar on the rue de l'École-de-Médicine. La Fourchette, it
was called, since then renamed Bistrot 1. In the heart of the
network, everyone had fake names. She called herself Sophie;
I don't know about him. She sometimes went to Brussels.
Did she carry messages? Money? The little attic studio where
she lived on the rue de l'Abbé-Groult, in the 15th arrondissement, was used as a mail drop and a hideout for Algerian
comrades.

She sheltered one called Black Mustapha. Afterward, she
learned that he was the head of the French federation of the
FLN. The man wasn't captured at her place but in another
pied-à-terre on the impasse de Deux-Anges in Saint-Germain-
des-Prés. In the course of an operation carried out during the
night on November 9 or 10, 1961, agents from the DST arrested
thirty or so activists. Basically the whole of the FLN leadership
in the city and around fifteen of their French supporters. The
next day, my parents went back to the rue de l'Abbé-Groult to
burn all the documents they found there. Convinced the police
were on their heels, they searched for a place to take shelter.

Luc thought of the in-between. Though the hole was much
too small to accommodate a couple, he'd cleaned it just in case.
He didn't really imagine hiding out steps from his mother's
bed. Certainly not with a woman whose meat was very fresh.
Alice Nuchi, a close friend of the family, offered to take them in.
They went to ground for two months in an attic loft she wasn't
using on the rue de la Folie-Méricourt. I came into the world
the following summer. If my calculations are correct, I must

have been conceived in what resistance and criminal jargon commonly calls a blind.

14

I succumb last. At least, that's how it seems. In the last scene, I'm half naked and stare into nothing, eating strips of flowered paper torn from the walls. A sheet thrown over a cradle covers what looks like the body of my little sister. I'm supposedly alone in the apartment. Our mother has disappeared. It's implied that she's been taken away in turn. Why she has decided to barricade herself at home, dying of starvation with her two children, is never explained.

At the beginning, everything seems normal. She pretends to wait for me in front of the school with Ariane, who is barely two. It's hot. Almost summer. I am among the children coming out of the courtyard in pairs. Because of the camera, they look at me like a curious creature. I blush to hear them whispering "he's an actor" behind my back. The satchel I wear across my chest is empty. My head is adorned with a Breton sailor's hat which I like to throw in the air on the way home.

My mother has barely closed the front door behind her when she locks it with boards and bolts, lowers the blinds, shuts the curtains, and serves dinner in front of the television, which only gives off a wavering, grainy image. Life goes on, as though nothing is happening. In the following days, she puts a birthday cake and presents down on the waxed tablecloth, then she reads a magazine, gives Ariane a bath in a plastic basin, looks at me absently, and makes faces at my sister.

Once her provisions are exhausted, her face becomes more solemn. She no longer gets up from her Formica chair. I jump up and down around her immobile body, I cry for food, return to the reflexes of a newborn. Close-up of me, trying to nurse at my mother's breasts, which are dry as old wells. Death arrives. You don't see it. It's enough to guess at its presence.

The filming took place in the Gabriel-Péri housing project in Saint-Denis. Christian had rented a two-bedroom apartment on the sixth floor of a public housing block. His first short films had been produced without any help. This time, he employed a small team—a cameraman, an assistant, a lighting guy—and a real script. Titled "Reconstruction of 45 Days before the Death of Françoise Guigniou," the work was inspired by a news feature, but it also reflected his own fears. Thanks to some money from the Centre National du Cinéma, he could have employed professional actors. To tell the story of this imprisonment, this household suicide, he preferred to use his own family.

15

My father built me a room in the attic, all the way in the back, past the statues with nails in them, the hanging knives, and Christian's metal instruments. A recess where the building extended on the back right side. Nearly its own pavilion, with a sloping finial and a square window. He did everything himself. The shelf. The loft where I slept. The wooden ladder that led to it. The trestle table. The sliding panel that served as a door. Exiled to the most remote part of the house, I was nearly at the deserted ends of the earth. At night, I heard a tawny owl crying from a neighboring garden. I felt like I was camping in one of the treehouses we made on vacation in Désertines.

In the glow of a clip-on lamp with a small metal shade, I kept going over the same scenario. I thought about ways to escape a nameless enemy. I waited for suspicious sounds in the courtyard, hatching increasingly convoluted plans to flee. I had

only one way out: the roof, which I could easily get to through
the window. From there, I imagined sliding down a gutter into
the park next door, with its trees full of nocturnal birds of prey.
I could also wait for assailants to enter the attic and fall into a
few traps before leaping across to the deck and running down
the stairs two at a time. There was one other option left: to
wall up the entrance to my room and provision myself through
a vent.

In their own ways, all of them tried to escape. Plunged into
silence, wayward in every ritual, iconoclastic and full of anach-
ronisms, that enclosed space generated ranks of cookie tins,
thousands of contact sheets, a few history books and studies
on phonetics or human relationships.

A part of me wished for a life without walls. If danger begins
on street corners, why not push farther? Once I crossed the
stoop, I felt capable of crossing any boundary. In the course
of my civil service, I left to live in Cairo. I worked for *Egyptian Progress*, a local paper that was as worn out as the cos-
mopolitan, Near Eastern, French-speaking world from which
it emerged.

The managing editor was a priest, mostly defrocked. An Italian who was almost one hundred and spent most of his time
feeding a horde of cats with morsels of soft food he scattered
all over the office. An Armenian pianist stood guard, with a
certain laxness, over the French language. The film critic was
half blind. A surgeon occupied his free time by responding to
mail from readers, and because most of these were dead or had
gone into exile, he filled his column with letters he wrote himself. The questions he hastily answered were mostly medical.

Three months after my posting, mère-grand came to visit

me with Jean-Élie and Anne. She was there and gone at the
same time. She sat rigid in the room of a grand, impersonal
hotel overlooking the Nile. Not agreeing or resisting. Passive
for the first time, as if she'd been removed from her body. A
pure spirit finally freed from her physical self.

Back then, the Egyptian telephone connection worked badly.
I could get messages from abroad, but I couldn't make calls.
To dial out of the country, I had to go to the post office in the
Mounira neighborhood, a place that was constantly packed,
overwhelmed by a deafening racket, and run by extremely
persnickety bureaucrats who handled their inked stamps like
weapons of war and sources of extra cash. One day I tapped out
the phone number of the Rue-de-Grenelle. On the other end
of the line, Jean-Élie told me in an arctic voice that his mother
was dead. Dead and buried weeks ago. No one had told me.

I don't know what sickness she succumbed to or if she suffered. When I returned to Paris, I found her room intact—but
empty of all human traces.

Acknowledgments

I wish to express my gratitude to Henri Nahum, who helped me to better understand the fate of Jewish doctors during the occupation, and to Frédéric Gugelot, whose work on the Catholic conversion of intellectuals was extremely helpful.

Manuel Carcassonne and Alice d'Andigné have my profound appreciation, as do Éric Aeschimann and François Reynaert.

Finally, I'd like to thank Emma, Anne, Ariane, Luc, Christian, and Jean-Élie for their help and their patience.

Translator's Note

Although this book is anchored in a very real place, it exists in a borderland between truth and fiction, the kind of space where definitions of genre sometimes force a divide. But a detective (or a player in Clue) can't investigate the past without imaginative work. As a translator, I wanted to respect the nuances of remembering the past in the present, the demand for both accuracy and curiosity, the direct examination of painful moments and the resourcefulness to approach them obliquely.

Like the fabric of memory, and of trauma, Christophe Boltanski's beautiful prose is made of hints, connections, triggers, and transitions that seem effortless but are carefully crafted. The setting is not just a series of images that create a mental picture. Instead, we are invited to develop a sustained spatial understanding that propels the narrative. In "Kitchen" Boltanski describes his grandmother moving across the house by leaning on pieces of furniture, "like carabiner hooks left for mountain climbers on a rocky slope." The writing also anchors itself from object to object as it moves toward the deepest part of the building.

The original French accomplishes this trajectory with a high level of detail that is always inventive. My challenge in English was to maintain the same balance of idiosyncrasy and smoothness that makes up Boltanski's meandering charm, at once leisurely and pointed, wide ranging and contained, hilarious and tragic. Within his vast vocabulary, each word builds on the previous one, transmuting rooms of the house into sections of the book.

The house itself resists translation—*hôtel particulier* means an aristocrat's in-town residence, which was noted in the social register. The Boltanskis don't just live in a fancy house in an upscale neighborhood, they live in a former nobleman's mansion, which has been divided up. Inside, the books on the shelves posed some difficulty because many of them have not been translated or are out of print. I've chosen to render the titles in English even when there isn't an English translation. For example, Myriam Boltanski's *Réanimensonge* becomes *Resucideception*. Many of these works are available online under the pseudonym Annie Lauran. If there is an English version, I use its title. This book also refers to two works by Georges Perec, which are both available in English—*Ellis Island* and *Species of Spaces*. I have slightly adapted the existing translation of the lines from *Ellis Island*.

In this very particular memory palace, I've attempted to preserve each sentence as a train of thought, reordering it as delicately as possible for the requirements of English syntax. Though the writing is precise, the descriptions of objects create something immaterial—the spirit of the house itself. In *The Poetics of Space*, Gaston Bachelard writes, "In its countless alveoli, space contains compressed time. That is what space is for." Opening these rooms requires a little speculating in the service of respect and preservation. Memory might be a novelist, but it is also a translator.

Translator's Acknowledgments

Thanks first of all to Christophe Boltanski for trusting me with his words and for patiently answering my many questions. I am grateful to the staff of the University of Chicago Press and to Alan Thomas for his commitment to the translation and for his excellent editorial sensibility. And thanks to my readers Elisa Gonzalez, Dolores Hayden, Lauren Roberts, Matt Kenyon, and especially Alice Kaplan, who has been so generous with her help and encouragement at every stage.